re

Boo
Fam
Faxi

F

CONVOY OF DEATH

Duncan Harding titles available from
Severn House Large Print

Clash in the Baltic
Hell on the Rhine
Ramps Down, Troops Away!
Sink the Hood
Slaughter in Singapore

CONVOY OF DEATH

Duncan Harding

Severn House Large Print
London & New York

This first large print edition published in Great Britain 2006 by
SEVERN HOUSE LARGE PRINT BOOKS LTD of
9-15 High Street, Sutton, Surrey, SM1 1DF.
First world regular print edition published 2005 by
Severn House Publishers, London and New York.
This first large print edition published in the USA 2006 by
SEVERN HOUSE PUBLISHERS INC., of
595 Madison Avenue, New York, NY 10022.

British Library Cataloguing in Publication Data

Harding, Duncan, 1926 -
  Convoy of death. - Large print ed.
  1. World War, 1939 – 1945 - Naval operations, British -Fiction
  2. World War, 1939 – 1945 - Naval operations, American - Fiction
  3. Great Britain - Foreign relations - United States - Fiction
  4. United States - Foreign relations - Great Britain - Fiction
  5. Great Britain - Foreign relations - 1936 – 1945 - Fiction
  6. United States - Foreign relations - 1933 – 1945 - Fiction
  7. War stories
  8. Large type books
  I. Title
  823.9'14 [F]

  ISBN-10: 0-7278-7512-4

Printed and bound in Great Britain by
MPG Books Ltd, Bodmin, Cornwall.

The worst voyage in the world
Winston Churchill, 1942

A Note From Duncan Harding

By now most of you, dear readers, know me for the old hack I am. I guess you've realized that scribblers like me are cynical old buggers. We're in this writing lark strictly for the money. We change our politics, principles, point-of-view like a cheap Nottingham whore changes her knicks – often.

For half a century now (it seems a lot longer, I can tell you), I've written about the lives of those good old boys who fought in the Big War for King and Country. Today many would say, more fool them, the silly old farts. But then patriotism is dead, a dirty word. And I can understand why when I listen to the lies of our political masters. No matter, I mustn't go off at a tangent, must I?

Naturally my publishers have pushed me into many of these 'tales of derring-do' to repeat the corny phrase they use, 'all thrills and spills'. Let me tell you there's not much of a thrill in getting a bullet shot up your rear end. But again I digress. The publishers, cunning devils that most of them are, promise money in hand and lots of royalties when the latest Harding epic has sold out; and of course I always fall for it, though naturally I need the dosh. With that new lady friend of mine – 'Madame de M&S', as she is known locally for her shopping habits – do I need cash!

What the publishers want is a 'good tale', set in a foreign location (exotic if possible), with a bit of juicy sex. If possible, they maintain, the good guys have to win over the bad 'uns. Mostly I can manage it. But as I grow older and ever more cynical it is becoming increasingly difficult to make the subjects of that poor stuttering king we had at that time come out on top.

However, to my surprise – and perhaps yours, gentle reader, this time I have come up with a subject that can't be bought or sold cheap. Even now as I write these lines of explanation on my battered old Olivetti (none of your newfangled technology for Duncan Harding), I am surprised at myself. How did it happen? Is it some form of senile dementia?

I don't know. All I *do* know is that you

can't sell cheap the fate of those who sailed the dreaded 'Murmansk Run', back in the years 1942 to 1944. It is recorded that ten thousand British merchant seamen, some as young as fourteen, left Hull for the Russian port in the Arctic Circle, never to return. With them went hundreds of Royal Naval ratings, manning the vessels that escorted those doomed convoys, who suffered a similar fate.

Most of them didn't stand a chance of surviving. Desperate to stop the Allied supplies of war reaching the hard-pressed Russians, the Germans pulled out all the stops to prevent the merchant ships and their naval escorts reaching Murmansk. The Jerries threw everything into the attack. As the Murmansk convoys sailed the length of German-occupied Europe, they attacked with everything from 50,000-ton battleships to tiny motor torpedo boats, plus the might of the Luftwaffe in Holland and Norway. If the truth be known, most of those brave young men, naval and civilian, were doomed from the moment they left the mouth of the Humber and began to sail north. If the Germans didn't get them, that cruel Arctic sea would.

Even the 'men' of the Royal Navy, who

made up most of the crews of the escorts, were really mere boys. 'HO men', as they were called, they were callow youths who, in most cases, had never even seen the sea before they were called up for the Navy.*

In their white 'art silk' mufflers, jaunty bell-bottoms and with the customary 'wood' (the cheap Woodbine cigarette) tucked behind their right ear, ready for a sly 'spit-and-a-draw', they rapidly outgrew the petty trivialities of their peacetime existence – pubs, pictures and palais-de-danse. For less than thirty bob a week, they willingly and knowingly risked their lives, well aware that they had a one in four chance of surviving. For many of them there would be no campaign medal to honour their courage in those dangerous frozen waters of the North Atlantic. Ironically enough it was the Russians who would grant them a 'gong' at the end of the long 'Cold War' of our own times.

No, even cash-strapped, cynical old hacks like yours truly couldn't just make money out of all that youthful courage and self-sacrifice. A few of them survived, as we shall see. Occasionally you see them among

*'Hostilities only'; men who had been called up for the duration of the war.

veterans of World War Two assembled at the Cenotaph, very old but smart and erect for the occasion in their blazers and bright white berets. People ask who are they in their unusual headgear. Nobody seems to know. Indeed, they are that terrible war's forgotten men. Perhaps my little tale might do something to rectify that.

D.H., Autumn 2004

Book One

A Call To Arms

One

The London train shuddered. It trembled. Steam poured from the locomotive. There was the rusty steel squeak of brake blocks. With a final violent judder, the long train came to a stop abruptly. From the racks, rifles, packs, suitcases, even sleeping small children, came tumbling down amid cries of alarm, curses, moans.

Hastily Sub-Lieutenant Horatio Smythe grabbed for the worn leather strap in the shabby first-class carriage to which he was now entitled – officer and gentleman. 'I say,' he exclaimed to the fat man opposite, who had kept his bowler on all the way from London, 'what's that?'

The fat businessman took the cigar out of his lips and told himself; Typical public school twerp, cannon fodder for the Murmansk Run probably. Still, he looks a nice sort of a lad with his clean-shaven cheeks,

15

unlined as yet, and bright blue innocent eyes. The poor sod doesn't know what he's in for. 'Routine, Lieutenant,' he said in his broad East Yorkshire accent. 'The military policemen always stop the train just before Hull Paragon Street. That's the only way they can catch the deserters. Once they're on the razzle at Paragon Street there's no catching those matelots of yours. The station's lousy with tarts. Sailors are always pretty quick at getting their feet under the table with some whore.' He took another complacent puff at his fat Havana as if he'd seen it all before and would probably see it all over again before the war was over.

Smythe's face coloured. 'You mean our chaps – *deserting*? I can't believe that, sir—'

'Get a load of that.' The fat businessman in the bowler cut him short. He pointed his cigar at the wet fields beyond. A sailor was running all out, pulling off his gas haversack as he did so, followed by two very tall Redcaps, crying for him to stop. 'You don't think he's going for a cross-country run, do you, Lieutenant?'

Smythe didn't answer. The bigger of the two Redcaps was drawing his pistol from its leather holster as he ran after the deserter. He gasped, 'He isn't going to shoot the

16

matelot, is he?'

The man in the bowler hat laughed. 'No, of course not. They're not shooting sailors yet. But the way things are going on the Murmansk Run, it won't be long, in my opinion, before they start doing so.'

The locomotive shuddered and ejected more steam into the damp morning air. The wheels clattered on the track. Slowly the London train began to move again, leaving the little group of quarry and pursuers behind. Smythe glanced at the poster stuck opposite, next to the faded travel poster advertising the delights of 'balmy Withernsea', wherever that was. It read 'Careless Talk Costs Lives'. Even as a very junior sub-lieutenant Smythe knew one should not talk about military affairs with 'civvies'. All the same he was intrigued by what he had just seen and the man in the bowler hat's references to the Murmansk Run. 'Why should they shoot sailors bound for the Murmansk Run if they attempt to desert, sir?'

The civilian looked at him pityingly as he folded the copy of the *Hull Daily Mail*, which he had bought at Doncaster half an hour before. 'Because that run to Russia is sheer hell – and the sailors know it. If the

17

Jerries don't get you, the freezing sea will. You go down to those dives in Hedon Road in Hull where the matelots hang out and listen to their tales. They'd make yer hair curl.' For a moment he raised his bowler to reveal he was completely bald, but there was no smile on his face as he did so. 'They say that already ten thousand of the poor buggers have been killed up there in the convoys. Once you've passed through the "Gate", as the sailors call it, and come back once, you're a lucky man. Do it twice, they say, and you've had all the luck you're ever going to have in this lifetime.' He paused and frowned grimly, as if he were just realizing what he had said.

Smythe realized that the man in the bowler had said all he was going to say, so he leaned back in the smelly plush seat, which looked as if it had not been cleaned since war had been declared three years before. Faintly he could hear above the clatter of the tracks the voice of the guard calling, 'All tickets please,' and the deeper voice of what was probably a military policeman ordering, 'All service personnel have yer paybooks and travel documents ready!' Smythe began to fumble inside his tunic for his own documents.

Two compartments away, in the third-class

18

section, Paddy Kerrigan, once known as Harold Smith, started to search for his own papers, feeling absolutely cool and in charge of the situation, as the fat sailor, who smelled of beer, turned in his sleep and tried to put his arms round him. It was the same in the packed carriage everywhere. They had jammed them in at King's Cross like sardines. There were even two ATS sleeping in the racks, one of them showing her khaki bloomers with careless abandon. Paddy told himself that the English rozzers wouldn't want to spend much time in his compartment. It stank of sweaty feet, stale beer and the cheap Hollywood Poppy scent from Woolworth's that the ATS were using. They'd do a bunk as soon as they could, and that was, Paddy told himself confidently, just as it should be.

The guard rapped on the door with his key and then slid it open, wrinkling his nose at the stink before growling, 'Tickets please.' Behind him the two hulking MPs, hands on their revolver holsters, waited, gimlet eyes under the peaks of their red caps flashing from one face to the other suspiciously. Paddy gave them his best Mick smile. They ignored it. For them, it seemed, everyone was guilty until he was proven innocent.

Swiftly the guard went through his routine and then the two policemen took over. It seemed they didn't notice the stink coming from the tightly pressed bodies of the third-class carriage; even the fat-legged ATS showing her khaki bloomers didn't worry them. They took their time, staring at each face as travel orders, passes and the like were presented, as if they were all a bunch of potential military criminals.

Paddy waited. As the only civilian in the carriage, Paddy knew that the military had no jurisdiction over him. But he wasn't going to let that worry him. He'd allow himself to be checked and questioned if necessary; that would make things easier. If he objected, he knew, they'd pull some trick to have him hauled off for further questioning in Hull station. Still, as they got closer to him he slipped his free hand into his trouser pocket and felt the comforting bulge of the little German pistol attached to his left leg by string. If it came to it, he told himself, he'd shoot.

'Civvy, eh?' the MP commented as he glanced hard at Paddy's papers, with the letter of reference on top of the work permit that Birch Builders had sent to him in Ireland. 'Mick?'

'Yes, your honour,' Paddy replied with a smile, giving them the full measure of the 'happy-as-pig-in-shit Irishman that Englishmen expected from the people they had enslaved and terrorized ever since the time of that bastard Cromwell. 'From County Sligo itself.'

The MP ignored the information. He said, 'You've got a reference letter from some Mick priest in York and this here work permit from the same place. How come?'

'How come what, sir?' Paddy asked, as polite as ever, though his overstrung nerves were now beginning to crackle electrically.

'Have you got cloth in yer ears?' the Redcap snapped roughly. 'You heard me. What connection do you have as a Mick with York?'

'God bless us and save us, sir,' Paddy replied with more relief than he felt. 'Why didn't you say so in the first place? The priest there, the good father, came from my own village, sir. Why he poured the holy water over me head when I was a babe. So he got me a job with his reference in this local firm. They're doing bomb-damage work in Hull. There's a great need of us paddies in Hull, sir, wherever that may be.'

His interrogator looked at the other

21

corporal. He nodded as if giving his approval. The first Redcap handed Kerrigan's papers back with, 'Well, watch yer step, Paddy, we've got our eyes on your kind. Keep yer nose clean, d'ye hear me?'

'Yes, sir,' he answered hastily, ever the willing stage-Irishman. 'Don't worry about me, sir, and God bless yer for your interest in a poor old Irish brickie.'

They passed on and Kerrigan felt the cold sweat trickle unpleasantly down the small of his back. Opposite him the fat ATS girl swung herself down from the luggage rack carelessly, showing even more of her khaki bloomers. 'Bastards!' she exclaimed to no one in particular. 'The Jerry Gestapo can't be worse than the sodding Redcaps.' There was a murmur of agreement among the others, while Kerrigan beamed at all and sundry as if he didn't have a care in the world...

The guard and the two Redcaps reached the last first-class carriage just as the train started to enter Hull's surburbs after its twelve-hour journey from King's Cross. At first there were the usual rows of new red-brick semis built in the '30s and sold for five hundred pounds or so to the petty clerks and minor managers who worked at Hull's docks. But the closer the train came to the centre of the north-eastern seaport, the more the houses lining the track seemed nothing more than a collection of ruins, abandoned, it seemed, to the bands of kids in ragged jerseys who played soldiers in the overgrown gardens and perhaps even lived in the Anderson shelters, which were everywhere. Here and there the ruins had vanished to be replaced by huge craters created by the seamines released by the German bombers that came over every night. It was a wasteland that Commander Donaldson thought worse than the damage created by the London Blitz of two years before.

He took his pipe out of his rotten teeth and rubbed the stem against his lemon-yellow cheeks and wondered what he had let himself in for now, just as the two Redcaps paused outside the door to his compartment and looked at the notice there, which read, 'Reserved for Senior Naval Officer'. They hesitated, but Donaldson waved his pipe at them and growled in his whisky voice, 'Well, come in if ye are coming in.'

The bigger of the two slid back the door, stood to attention and saluted. 'Didn't know whether we should disturb you, sir ... We're coming into Paragon Street in a minute as it is, sir.'

'Ye no disturbing me, Corporal.' He pushed his papers at the Redcap, adding, 'My shit nae smells any better than anyone else's.'

The Redcap actually blushed. Hastily he examined the papers and, handing them back as the train began to slow, whispered to his mate, 'Yon's a hard bugger.'

The Redcap was right. Commander D. O. Donaldson, DSO, DSC, was a 'hard bugger'. Now as he flung open the door and prepared to step on to the platform, eyes red and fierce, glaring all around at the bustling platform, packed with sailors and soldiers returning to their duties, he took the silver flask containing proof whisky from the pocket of his tunic. With a flamboyant gesture, he unscrewed the cap, poured himself a dram and tossed it back with a grunt, followed by a shudder and a licking of his parched lips.

It was a deliberate gesture, calculated to upset anyone watching who thought that senior naval officers shouldn't drink in this manner in public. Donaldson didn't give a damn. He had burned his boats long ago. What did he care what people thought of him? The powers that be needed him at the moment – they'd never sack him, even if he sank a battleship. Once the war was over – and if he survived – they'd have him out of the Royal Navy in three shakes of a lamb's tail. So why worry?

Standing on the platform waiting for the new skipper of the minesweeper HMS *Black Swan*, known all along the east coast as the *Mucky Duck*, Chief Petty Officer Alf Tidmus groaned when he saw Lieutenant Commander Donaldson. 'Holy mackerel,' he cursed under his breath in that flat Holderness accent of his, 'it's Drunken Doug! Just my frigging luck.'

Then, straightening up his skinny old shoulders and feeling the comforting warmth of the wintergreen plaster his wife had slapped on his bony back half an hour before, he advanced upon his new skipper, saluted and snapped in best Royal Navy fashion, 'Chief Petty Officer Tidmus, sir, from the *Black Swan*, sir.'

Donaldson breathed out hard, filling the air with the smell of whisky. 'Chiefie,' he said, and returned the petty officer's salute casually. 'Know you, don't I, Chiefie. Narvik 1940?'

'That's right, sir. Hairy that, sir,' he said cheerfully. Under his breath, he told him-

25

self, 'The old bugger's got a good memory, still. Forgets he nearly got us all sunk then up that frigging Norwegian fiord.' He bent down to pick up the commander's bag.

Donaldson stopped him with an urgent wave of his hand. 'Leave it, Chiefie. One of yon braw women porters can deal with it.' He indicated the nearest woman porter, pushing her trolley, enormous breasts ready to burst out from beneath her LNER waistcoat at any moment. 'We'll head for the nearest watering hole – one that's still got some whisky. I'll buy you a pint and you can fill me in on this bloody old *Black Swan* of yourn.'

Inwardly Tidmus groaned. The old soak was up to his bloody tricks already. Aloud he said, 'There's the bar of the Queen's Hotel just to the right – over there, sir. They'll have whisky.'

Donaldson's red eyes glittered for a moment. 'Well, better not waste time, Chiefie. There's a war to be won, you know. Lead on, McDuff.'

Tidmus 'led on'.

Two

Sub-Lieutenant Smythe was a little shocked. He had been in London from Dartmouth a couple of times since the Blitz and had seen the ruins of the centre of the capital. Hull, however, came as a complete surprise; he had not expected so much damage. Hull had always been for him the BBC's 'north-eastern port that was raided last night'. He had not been able to visualize just how much that 'north-eastern port' had suffered,

'Not a pretty picture,' the civilian in the bowler hat commented, catching the look in the young officer's eyes.

'No, I'd not expected this,' Smythe agreed, staring around at the brick wasteland outside Paragon Street station.

'Well, ever since the Russians came into the war and Churchill has been supplying them from here, Old Jerry has been knocking the stuffing out of the place. Hull, right on the coast, makes an easy target for their bombers from Norway and Holland.' He grinned and rammed his bowler more tightly on his bald head as the wind came in straight off the Humber estuary just at the end of the road. 'All you southerners know about the place is that the Humber is the arsehole of the world and Hull is stuffed right up.' He said the words in a matter-of-fact tone and without rancour. All the same, Smythe flushed, as if the bombing of Hull was his fault in some way.

Suddenly the man in the bowler reached out and patted his shoulder, 'Look after yersen, lad,' he said. 'Have a good time while you can. There are plenty ladies of easy virtue in Hull—' He broke off as if he realized he was embarrassing the young officer, who was barely out of his teens. 'Best of luck.' Then he was submerged into the crowd of soldiers and sailors, even before a red-faced Smythe could utter his thanks.

For a moment or two Smythe stood there, indecisive, wondering what he should do next, though he knew he had to report to the naval authorities by eighteen hundred hours that night. All around servicemen surged out into the growing winter gloom. There was the usual hustle and bustle of a wartime station: self-important railway transport officers striding up and down with their check-boards; Redcaps in pairs on the lookout for deserters; whores idling in the shadows, calling 'Like a nice time, soldier? Ten bob'; streams of pale-faced sickly looking sailors, caps on the backs of their heads, Woodbines behind their ears, silk mufflers thrown dashingly around their necks, heading for the blue-painted buses that would take them down to their ships and the docks – all of them, officials, cops, whores, sailors, caught in the terrible killing machinery of the Murmansk Run.

'Begging your pardon, your honour?'

The voice, obviously Irish, caught him completely by surprise. He turned, startled. A smiling man in his late-twenties, dressed in a shabby jacket and cap, with blue overalls underneath and a leather toolbag slung over his shoulder, was facing him, his gaze radiating warmth and good-humoured tolerance. 'Yes?' Smythe asked.

'I wonder if your honour would be knowing this place?' The stranger held up a piece of crumpled paper with a letterhead he couldn't quite see and said, 'It's somewhere round here, I have been told, sir. I hope so, cos these tools weigh a ton.' His smile broadened even more.

'Hedon Road.' Smythe read the name of the street, hearing it for the second time this grey wartime afternoon.

Again the young officer blushed. He was doing it all the time, with officers, cocky ratings, girls – especially with girls – now even with this friendly, smiling, lost Irishman. Why, Smythe didn't know; all he wished was that he wouldn't. Blushing was damned embarrassing. 'I'm afraid I don't know where it is,' he said apologetically. 'All I know it's somewhere nearby. I heard it this very afternoon.'

The Irishman took it in good part. 'Now don't you go worrying, sir,' he said and stuck the paper back in his overalls. 'I'm sure I'll find it. The top of the day to you, sir. Goodbye.' And with that he had disappeared into the mob, crossing the packed street to where another one led to the estuary and the docks.

Smythe dismissed the smiling Irishman and concerned himself with his own affairs. He would have dearly liked to have gone into the bar of the hotel and ordered a shandy – he hadn't had a drink of anything since they had left King's Cross at four o'clock that morning. But mummy wouldn't have liked him to go drinking – she was very against the 'strong waters' save at Christmas – and, besides, bars and their brassy cheeky barmaids frightened him and made him blush too.

Abruptly the young officer realized that for virtually the first time in his short life he was alone; that he had to start making decisions for himself. At boarding school and then at Dartmouth others had made those decisions for him. Always his days had been planned for him and he had not been encouraged to decide for himself. Now he was alone in a great bombed city and soon he would be commanding men, mostly older than himself. Soon he would have to take life by the scruff of the neck and make it do what *he* wanted. It was a frightening thought. He shivered and it wasn't the cold evening breeze coming off the sea that made him do so; it was the thought of what was to come, once he went to sea. God, why hadn't he joined the army like his mummy had wanted him to instead of following his dead father into the Royal Navy?

But there was no turning back now, Smythe knew that. He had to move on, come what may. Fighting back the tears that had suddenly flooded his eyes, he walked quickly over to the rank of ancient taxis waiting for customers outside the hotel...

The dockies were coming off shift now. Heading straight for the pubs that lined Hedon Road, they had little time for the two naval persons stumbling and tripping over the gear they had dropped carelessly on the quays as soon as the sirens had signalled the end of their shift.

CPO Tidmus cursed them as they flew by him in the growing darkness, lighting their stolen cigarettes as they ran, trying not to lose the looted foodstuffs they had hidden in their jackets and overalls.

'Bloody bolshy dockies,' Tidmus grumbled. 'Ten quid a week they get, while our blokes are lucky if they get ten bob, and still they cry stinking fish all the time, ready to down tools and strike at a moment's notice, sir.'

Commander Donaldson, a little unsteady on his feet now after six swift doubles at the station hotel, didn't seem to notice. As they came closer to the mooring, his gaze was fixed exclusively on the *Black Swan*, his new command.

Realizing that the new skipper wasn't listening to his customary complaints about the dockers, CPO Tidmus said, 'You can see she's no oil painting, sir. But don't worry, sir, she's a lot tougher than she looks. She's survived nearly three years of war.'

'Hm,' Donaldson grunted and wished he could drink another dram. The *Black Swan* certainly was no oil painting, that was for sure. Everywhere her hull was specked with red rust, and her two tall funnels were covered by peeling zigzag camouflage paint. 'Yon ship looks as if she'd just been bluidy well salvaged from the bottom of the sea,' he commented drily.

Tidmus gave a hollow laugh. 'Well, sir, she was once after Dunkirk two years ago. They gave her a coat of paint then.'

'Aye, and not another since then, Chiefie.'

'Very probably, sir,' Tidmus agreed. Over the estuary the searchlights were already probing the darkness with their icy fingers. The air-raid sirens would be sounding at any minute now, Tidmus told himself. Old Jerry recced the docks for new convoys setting sail for Murmansk every night. 'But, as I say, she's a good old craft.'

'So you say, Chiefie,' Donaldson said without conviction. 'But we can soon tidy up her superstructure. Their Lordships –' he meant the Admiralty – 'can surely afford to pay for a few pots of paint. It's the rest of her that worries me.'

'How do you mean, sir?' Tidmus asked, as, over in Patrington, not far from the exit to the Humber estuary, the first siren started to sound its shrill warning. The German night bombers were on their way.

'Well, how damned seaworthy is she?' Donaldson growled. 'She looks like a bunch of scrap to me.'

'She's not that bad, sir,' Tidmus replied. 'She's seen a lot of action—'

'It shows.'

Tidmus, who was proud of the old ship, ignored the commander's words. He said, 'The old *Mucky Duck* takes nothing from the sea, sir. She sort of wiggles up on old Jerry, does what she has to do and sneaks off again. If you was to ask me, sir, it's not old Jerry who's the main enemy of the ship, it's the bloody North Sea.' He broke off abruptly. Over to the east the fort anchored off Spurn Point had begun firing. Scarlet stabs of anti-aircraft fire split the lowering grey sky. 'I think we'd better be getting under cover, sir. The air-raid shelters in Hedon Road'll be packed soon. And it ain't safe here on the docks.'

For the moment Donaldson ignored the comment. Instead he took a long look at the old battered minesweeper and then said, 'We've got the rest of this month to get her shipshape and Bristol fashion, Chiefie. The new crew'll have the same time to settle down as well.'

'Sir. But remember, sir, they'll be a draft straight from Pompey. Most of them HO men won't ever have been to sea before. We'll have a job on our hands with them young matelots.'

'I have every confidence in you, Chiefie. An old seadog like you'll soon knock 'em into shape. And you've got my full authority to do any bloody thing you like with 'em.' He lowered his voice. 'You see, Chiefie, this time the convoy we'll be escorting'll be something special.' He looked to left and right, as if he were afraid he might be overheard. Over on the other side of the estuary at Immingham the great German basket flares – 'Christmas trees', the German pilots called them – came floating down with stately grace, illuminating all below them in a brilliant incandescent white light.

'Special, sir? On the Murmansk Run?'

'Yes, and don't you dare, Chiefie, tell anyone, even your missus, what I'm going to tell you now. If you do, I'll have your guts for garters, chief petty officer or not.'

35

'Yessir. I understand.'

'Well it's this. We're going to escort a convoy of Yanks, the first Yanks to tackle the Murmansk Run. It's going to be a propaganda exercise worked out by Roosevelt and Uncle Joe,' he said, referring to the Russian dictator. 'Naturally Churchill's behind it. He wants to take the pressure off our merchant navy and show the Yanks what kind of losses we're taking on these trips to Russia. I should imagine it's all really to do with the Second Front. As you know Roosevelt wants to attack over the Channel into France this year. You know, I know, we're in no position to do so, Roosevelt will back off and the invasion of Europe can wait another year or so.'

CPO Tidmus looked puzzled. 'But how can a convoy to Murmansk affect the Second Front, sir?'

Donaldson laughed. It wasn't a pleasant sound. 'How? Easy. Let the Yanks suffer the same kind of losses we've been suffering this last year and they'll soon have second thoughts. So far they've had a cushy war with us doing their fighting for 'em. Now let the Yankee buggers start paying the butcher's bill in men and ships and then they'll see things a bit different.'

CPO Tidmus looked aghast. He had never thought of the war in those terms before. Churchill was going to sacrifice American lives to get his way with the planned invasion of France. 'But doesn't that mean, sir,' he stuttered, finding it hard to put his confused thoughts into words, 'if the Yanks are going to take bad casualties on this Murmansk so soon, we in the escorts are going to do the same?'

But Lt Commander Donaldson didn't seem to have an answer for that overwhelming question.

Three

Paddy Kerrigan took a last bite of the stale bread and dripping. He'd thought that Kilmartin's boarding house on Hedon Road would mean that the tumbledown place would be run by Irish folk like himself. He had been mistaken. They had been Irish all right, but from Ulster and, like all those Protestant bastards up north, they were as mean as sin; they would not give you the muck from beneath their fingernails. Hence his 'supper', although he had surrendered his ration book to them, had been a weak cup of milkless, sugarless cocoa and stale bread and dripping. 'Bad cess on yer,' he had cursed underneath his breath when he had seen the evening fare. Aloud he said, the jovial Irishman as always, 'God bless you, Mrs Kilmartin, I haven't seen the like of that kind o' beef dripping since the war started and me old Aunt Kathleen died, God rest her soul.'

Now he swallowed the bread and stared out at the blacked-out street, with the ships beyond outlined a stark black by the fires already raging on the Lincolnshire side of the estuary. He smiled, a real one now, for the first time this day. The Germans were doing a good job. Already he could see a tanker burning furiously in mid-Channel, with the waterborne fire hoses failing to make any impression on the oil. He told himself that the burning tanker would make an ideal marker for the next flight of Junkers coming from Spurn Point. 'Give 'em hell, lads,' he cried enthusiastically, as the bombs continued to crash down despite the flak coming up in red-and-white fury from both sides of the Humber. Then as an after-thought, a bit of a joke, he raised his right hand as he had seen them do in Berlin and added, 'Heil Hitler.'

He yawned suddenly. It had been a long day and abruptly he felt very tired. Even the sagging old mattress, specked with the red marks of bed bugs, looked inviting. At that moment he felt he could sleep for ever. All the same he observed the routine and discipline they had taught him at the spy school at Wohltorf, just outside Hamburg.

The door was locked already. But that wasn't enough. Locks could be easily picked. So he wedged the one rickety chair the room possessed underneath the handle. Then, walking backwards from the door, he spread his copy of the *War Cry*, which he had picked up from the Salvation Army in the pub down below, carefully on the floor till he reached the brass bedstead. Satisfied, he pulled the string to which the pistol was attached from inside his trouser leg, untied the knot and placed the gun underneath his dirty pillow. The *Abwehr* had trained him well in such security matters, but ever since he was a kid and the tragedy which had struck his family had changed his whole life, he had known the importance of the gun. In the last resort it was always better to die with a weapon in your hand than to dangle tamely at the end of a length of English hemp.

Now he crawled into the bed keeping his shirt on and his shoes handy – just in case. He lit his last Woodbine and lay there, hands underneath his head, smoking fitfully, watching the blue smoke ascend slowly to the cracked dirty ceiling. Outside the Junkers had done all the damage they could do this night before the English fighters were scrambled on their Yorkshire fields. Now they were heading back to their bases on the Continent, fired at by the flak as they roared down the Humber.

He was tired. Yet he couldn't quite drop off. As always, he couldn't shake off the memories. Sometimes a woman helped. (Down below he could hear the squeak of an old bed as some sailor rogered one of the whores who were everywhere at this time of night on Hedon Road and he knew he could have bought a woman easily – a port-and-lemon, a packet of fags and ten bob and she'd be his for half an hour.) But this night he didn't feel the urge. His mind was full of his youth and his new mission...

He had been barely ten when the Black

and Tans had murdered his father. There had been four of them, armed with heavy German automatics. They had worn the funny mixed uniform that gave them their nickname in Southern Ireland and there was no mistaking them for veterans of the trenches of the war in France, which had just ended. Two of them, both with their Balmorals pulled well down over their eyes, had come in through the front door, the other two had covered the back and the windows.

His father had put up a good show, though his terrified son had seen he was afraid as the men hit him a couple of times across the face before starting to question him. 'Me in the Movement?' he had protested. 'One of the boys? With a name like Smith and a Protestant to boot. Why should a fellah like me help those Roman Candle bastards?'

They hadn't believed his father. Some bastard of a government nark had fingered him. They knew who his father was all right and what he did for the Movement. At first they played with the old man. They punched him a bit – they always did – made fun of his accent, called him a 'Paddy pig farmer', and then they'd found the poteen, a whole quart of the potent liquor. That had done it; they'd turned brutal and sadistic.

They'd ripped his dad's shirt off to reveal the skinny, hard-worked body beneath and had begun pressing the glowing ends of their 'gaspers', as they called their cigarettes, against his flesh. Time and time again, all the while passing the bottle from one to another, taking hefty swallows until their faces were flushed an ugly red.

In the end his dad had told them what they had wanted to know about the local boyos hiding out in the nearby hills. Hiding in the attic, peering through the gaps in the boards at the terrible scene being played out in the light of a lantern below, he had thought his father was going to get away with it.

That wasn't to be.

As the two of them backed off, leaving the old man kneeling on the floor, moaning softly, the bigger of the two, in a black shiny mackintosh, had raised his Mauser and said in what he probably thought was a kindly voice, 'Well we'll be going, Mr Smith and good Protestant as you are.' Almost casually he'd pressed his trigger.

The big pistol had jumped in his hand, but at that range he couldn't miss. The 9mm slug had propelled his father backwards, as if someone had slammed a giant fist into him. He had slapped against the wall, with all the cups tumbling out of his dead mother's dresser above him. His dad had been stone dead among the broken crockery and Waterford glass a minute later. The big Black and Tan had laughed as he had closed the door.

A week later, red faced, shaken, given to frequent tears but burning with a desire for revenge, he had gone out to kill the first English soldier he met. The boyos had laughed when he had asked for a 'cannon', but in the end, seeing how serious the little tousle-haired boy in short pants was, they had given him one and shown him how to use it – not that he had needed to be taught. He had walked down the cobbled street into the village, where there were English soldiers everywhere. But they had all looked so tough and on the alert, their upper bodies festooned with leather bandoliers of ammunition, grenades stuck in their belts, that he had had second thoughts every time he thought he might kill one of them.

In the end he knew it had to be Algie, as he was called, even by the sullen villagers. Everyone knew Algie. He was drunk most of the time, even when he was guarding the bridge that joined the two halves of the village together, and, whether he was on the drink or not, he was friendly to the locals. He'd give pennies and sweets to the ragged barefoot kids and call the old biddies with their shawls over their heads 'Ma' and never bothered to search the young men, which he should have done. Most of the time the locals couldn't understand what he was saying, his Yorkshire accent was so thick, but they all knew 'Old Algie', as they called him, meant them no harm. For half the time he was drunk and the other blinking his eyes to fight off sleep.

Thus it had happened. While the boyos, drinking their porter, or illegal poteen, had stared out of the window of the Phoenix pub, and the old biddies, hiding their weather-beaten faces with their scarves, had watched from the shadowed doorways of their cabins, he had walked up to the old soldier with his walrus moustache almost casually. Algie had been at the beer again and he was leaning against the stone balustrade of the bridge, bayoneted rifle gripped between his knees, fighting off sleep the best he could.

The old soldier had smiled at him and then he had staggered to his sentry box, placed his rifle down and had brought out a bar of Fry's peppermint cream chocolate. 'Here you are, son,' he said. 'A nice bar—' Algie had broken off suddenly, as he saw the revolver in the boy's hand. But he showed no fear. Hadn't he faced an attack by the Prussian Guard on the Somme? 'Now come on, son,' he managed to say. 'Don't lark around.'

It was then that he had pressed the trigger. The weapon barked and jerked upwards in his hand. For a moment he had thought he had missed, for the old soldier had shown no sign of being hit. But he hadn't missed. Slowly, very slowly, as if in slow motion, Algie's legs had begun to sag beneath him. A strange animal-like moaning had come from deep within him. Dark red blood had seeped, from the left side of his abruptly gaping mouth, running through his stained grey 'tea-strainer' moustache. With shocking suddenness Algie had gone down on his knees, face contorted with pain and surprise, turned upwards as if begging for mercy from some god on high. But God was looking the other way this cold grey day in Ireland. It was a look that the boy would never forget.

But now panic seized him. He should have thrown away the revolver; he knew that from the boyos and his dead father. But he didn't. Instead he was running for his life, the hot pistol clutched to his chest, while the boyos in the Phoenix applauded and one of the old biddies slipped slyly from her doorway to grab the dying man's rifle and his leather bandolier of ammunition for the Movement...

The Movement had taken care of him thereafter. They had given him a good Irish name instead of the hated English one. He had become Paddy Kerrigan and been given the papers that went with it. Now school had been out of the question. Instead he had been trained in the use of arms, to act as a lookout and spy – who would suspect a round-faced kid in short pants of working for the boyos? They even had allowed him to work on setting up an ambush for Michael Collins, the traitor. But after that particular killing, Southern Ireland had been too hot to hold those who were remotely connected with the murder of the Movement's one-time hero. He had been moved north to Ulster with the rest of them. Naturally the RUC had been looking for them as well as the Garda and for a while it had been intended he should be sent to Boston. But in the end the Movement had decided on something else for him.

As the Chief had explained it, in the last war the Germans had helped the Movement with gold, arms and men from the Irish Brigade. Now Imperial Germany had vanished and the new Germany was a defeated country, dominated by the English and the other allies. But Germany's time would come again, the Chief had maintained, and there were those in that country who had always helped the Movement to throw off the English yoke and unite the whole of Ireland. He had to help to maintain those contacts with Germany.

Thus it was that as a boy of fourteen, disguised as a cabin boy on a Yankee ship, whose captain was a friend of the Movement, and armed with two pristine white five-pound notes – worth a fortune in defeated Germany – he had made contact in Hamburg with those in that country who would change his whole life and be responsible so many years later for his being here in Kilmartin's rundown boarding house in a ruined Hull this very night...

Four

'Well, luv,' his wife said, pausing with her broom in her hand, 'how did the day go?'

CPO Tidmus looked down at the broken glass that his wife was attempting to sweep up by the light of a torch strapped to her forehead underneath the iron curlers. He didn't answer the question. Instead he asked one of his own. 'Not the ruddy front window again?'

She nodded and switched off the torch; batteries were hard to come by even on the dockyard's black market. 'I've talked to them Irish navvies doing the repairs up the road. They say they'll send a glazier tomorrow morning at eight sharp. The government'll pay.'

'Yeah and you'll be using up our tea ration all morning feeding the glazier bugger cups of char,' Tidmus growled and followed his wife into their little house, crunching over the glass broken in the night's air raid.

'There's no bloody end to the bloody bombing.'

'None of that swearing,' she warned a little wearily, 'you're not on your boat now.'

'*Ship*,' he corrected her routinely as he had done over thirty years of married life. He took off his cap and gas mask and opened his too-tight tunic with a sigh of relief before settling down in his favourite chair as she bustled off into the pantry to bring his evening jug of stout.

'Ta,' he said, as she poured him a glass of the beer. 'You're not a bad old stick for a married woman.' He took a pleasurable sip of the precious liquid. 'I mean, it's your single woman who's usually out to please a bloke. *And*,' he paused significantly, giving her a pat on her ample bottom, 'give him a bit o' the other.'

She dodged his second pat neatly and said, 'You get yer share of it.'

'But only on Saturday night and when I come back from sea.'

She ignored the comment and started pouring the scalding hot water from the kettle on the coke fire, ready for him to soak his corns, which he usually did when he had had a hard day. 'What was the new lot like, Alf?'

He shrugged. 'The usual bunch of HO blokes, still wet behind the ears, and a couple of three-stripers, who'll do just enough to keep them out of trouble and no more. That's why they're three-stripers after serving in the Royal since bleeding Nelson's day.'

'Language,' she warned him again routinely. 'And the new skipper?'

He paused, his wrinkled old brow creased in thought. 'Don't know exactly, Aggie,' he said slowly. 'He's a bloke called Donaldson. A Scot that us old hands call Drunken Doug – he likes his booze, you see.'

'Look who's talking,' she said, putting yesterday's *Hull Daily Mail* on the hearth in front of the fire in case he splashed.

'He's a brave bugger, of course. DSC and FSC, one in the old war and one in this – at Narvik in '40.'

'I remember,' she said, knowing how she had worried so much while he had been away during the first battle of Narvik and the Germans were sinking everything right up to aircraft carriers along the Norwegian coast. 'But what else?'

CPO Tidmus began taking off his boots, feeling the stiffness in his skinny back again, despite the brand new wintergreen plaster from the chemist she'd slapped on it that very morning.

'I don't rightly know, Aggie,' he answered slowly. 'Something went wrong when he was out in the Med. They'd given him a destroyer about the time of the Battle of Crete in '41, you know when we lost all those destroyers trying to get the Army blokes off Crete when the Jerries invaded. Anyhow, he must have dropped a clanger out there because by this time, with his seniority and experience, he ought to have been given a cruiser by their Lordships. Instead he's bin given command of the old *Mucky Duck*. Not that there's anything wrong with her, Aggie.'

'I know ... I know,' she said soothingly. 'Everybody knows that the sun shines out of her arse, Alf Tidmus.' She grinned.

He did, too, his seriousness vanished at once. 'Now where did you hear language like that, Aggie. It'd make even a hardened matelot blush.'

'Now where indeed? Now drink yer ale and do yer feet so we can get yer into kip and rest yer weary old bones. It's gonna be another long day again tomorrow.'

'That it is, Aggie lass,' he agreed, telling himself that an old beat-up sailorman like him didn't deserve someone like his Aggie.

He drank his stout, as she had commanded, and felt a happy man...

Some miles away the newest crew member of the *Mucky Duck*, as he already knew they called the rusty old tub of a minesweeper in which he now found himself, thought he'd never get to sleep. Horatio Smythe was in his 'cabin', a cold, clammy, smelly steel tank without even a porthole, separated from the corridor outside solely by a blackout curtain. Not that one was really needed. Like everything else that he had come across in the minesweeper so far the electricity didn't seem to work properly. It flickered off and on all the while and his new skipper, a surly, tough-looking Scot, seemed too drunk to notice and have something done about it.

Indeed the only one aboard who did appear efficient was the venerable chief petty officer, who smelled of menthol, who had shown him round. 'Chiefie', as everyone, even the ratings, called him, even seemed to be proud of the old tub. He went into detail about the ship's machinery – 'engine, 1,200 HP Triple Expansion, sir,' he had explained to a somewhat bemused Horatio, 'big enough to power a large freighter, sir ... Range twenty days under full power, sir,' he had added proudly, 'though we did go one day over that on our last Murmansk Run.'

That 'Murmansk Run' had caught Smythe's attention. *Murmansk*. It seemed to him to be on everyone's tongue in the short time that he had been in the Hull area. He would have dearly loved to have asked more questions about those trips to northern Russia, which seemed to worry even the toughest of these veteran old seadogs. But he decided to keep his mouth shut, working on the assumption that he'd hear more than enough about them in the days to come. For just before Chiefie had finished his little lecture about the rusty old tug, he had remarked, 'It looks, sir, as if we've got a couple of weeks to work the *Black Swan* up for action, according to the captain.'

'Action?' he had queried. 'Where?'

By way of an answer, the old CPO had jerked his thumb over his shoulder in the direction of north and Smythe had understood immediately what he had meant. The *Black Swan*, too, was going on one of those feared Murmansk runs.

Now as he lay in his hard bunk, listening to the drip-drip of a leaking pipe close by, Smythe, unable to sleep, worried and wondered how he would fare in his first action, for he guessed that the convoys that ran north to Russia would be subjected to intense enemy activity, especially as they ran the length of German-occupied northern Europe once they had left the safety of Scotland. They'd be attacked right along the coasts of Holland and Norway until they came into the Russian-controlled area. Germany, he knew from the papers, was fighting for its life in Russia. The enemy would do his damndest to prevent supplies reaching the Russians.

Not that the young officer felt afraid for himself. But he *was* afraid of showing fear in front of others, if his nerve broke and he couldn't control himself when under attack. Like all young men of the time he had been subjected to bombing on a couple of occasions and although he hadn't been particularly worried about his own safety – like all young men he felt death happened to someone else – he had jumped nervously when bombs had exploded or the anti-aircraft guns had fired close by. But as an officer he had to set an example to those under his command – that had been drummed into him time and time again at the Royal Naval College. Officers must not show fear. But when the time came would he be able to control himself?

Then, when he despaired he would never sleep, concerned as he was about his own problem, he remembered the old chiefie's words after the surly captain had dismissed them earlier on with, 'Well, you're young even for a ruddy snotty, laddie. But I suppose you'll do, you'll have to do like the rest of this ruddy gash crew o' mine.'

Outside CPO Tidmus had said, when they were out of earshot, 'If I may say so, sir, if you need any help – well, I'll allus be glad to do the best I can for you, sir. And don't pay no heed to the skipper. He's old school ... His bark is worse than his bite.' And Tidmus had smiled at him in an almost fatherly fashion, showing his ugly yellow false teeth. It had been then that Smythe had realized he had gained an ally.

Now the pressure relaxed in the knowledge that CPO Tidmus would look after him if necessary. He yawned and, turning wearily on his side, closed his eyes. Tomorrow he'd write to Mummy in Bournemouth and tell her he had found a good ship with a good crew and that he was settling in nicely. It would ease the poor dear's mind – since Pater's death she had been very nervous and quickly given to tears; she always worried about him so much. And he'd entitle her letter, although it wasn't strictly true, 'On Active Service'. The censor wouldn't mind, he supposed. The thought pleased him. Five minutes later he was fast asleep, snoring gently as if he hadn't a care in the world. That night his dreams would be full of an innocent boy's idea of glory...

Now only the men on watch and Commander Donaldson remained awake, as over in Hull the pubs and the dives closed and the shore patrols and the police, patrolling Hedon Road in pairs, ushered the drunks, the pimps, the whores and the good-time girls who would do 'it' in a doorway standing up, their cheap frocks up above their naked waists for half a crown, back to their ships and homes. Another grey day in the middle of a grey war had come to a close and Hull fell asleep.

Donaldson, as drunk as he was – and by this time of the night he was always drunk, even when he was on duty – knew, however, that that was not strictly the case. In George Street where naval headquarters was located, the staff of the Flag Officer In Charge, Hull, would be working out all their fates. Hard-faced old salts, too old now to be given a command, and resenting it, and smart young officers who belonged to the 'Wavy Navy'* and were only too glad to be safe 'on the beach' would be hard at it, planning routes, distances, daily sail-mileage, position of aircraft and convoy-protection ships. Naturally all of them knew that the convoy would meet with disaster; they always did. Time and time again the convoys would set out in high hope, believing that this time they would outwit the Hun. But they never did. The Hun always had something new up his sleeve and the convoys suffered accordingly.

Donaldson sighed as he lay on his bunk, toying with his last glass of whisky for this night. He knew that Churchill had called the Murmansk Run 'the worst voyage in the world'. Old Winnie didn't know the half of it. The men who sailed those ships, those who survived, had another description: 'hell below zero'. And they were right. The matelots of the Royal Navy and the men of the Merchant Navy fought not only the German enemy, but also the murderous elements: Arctic winds that whipped a look-

*The Royal Navy Volunteer service, whose officers bore wavy gold stripes instead of the straight ones of the regular Royal Naval officer.

out's face into the colour of an underdone steak; icy waters that froze the torpedoed sailor to death within seconds; frozen metal that ripped the flesh off the men's hands in bloody chunks if they were foolish enough to touch it without gloves.

Of such things Donaldson himself had no fear. His life was forfeit as it was and there was no future for him. All the same, the old habits of duty and purpose died hard. He wanted to make a success of this last convoy, even though he knew it would not advance his career one iota, and that the whole business was regarded as a public relations exercise for the bloody Yanks by those cynics in Whitehall.

'Show 'em, Doug,' he whispered to himself, talking to himself in the manner of lonely men. 'Show 'em what ye can do with a battered old sieve of a ship and a crew that is basically a shower of shit.' He took another drink of the precious whisky. 'Aye,' he said, 'ye can do it, that ye can, man.' He finished off the rest with a flourish. The glass fell to the deck from his suddenly lifeless fingers. He rolled to one side, still fully dressed apart from his boots, and lay absolutely still, his eyes closed, not making a single movement. To any observer entering his cabin at that moment, Donaldson would have seemed, to all intents and purposes, to be already dead...

Five

CPO Tidmus had warned them. He'd addressed them in the mess deck the night before. He knew his matelots and didn't want to lay it on too thick – that would start them with a grievance against the new skipper, for sailors were sensitive souls. All the same he felt it his duty as the senior petty officer and in a way a kind of liaison man between the skipper and the lower-deck ratings to warn them about Commander Donaldson and his legendary hot temper. 'Now listen, you ratings, especially you HO blokes. The new captain takes over command officially tomorrow and before we start working up exercises for what's to come –' he had felt it not necessary at that moment to detail what was to come; they'd find that out soon enough – 'the skipper'll take a good look at the old *Mucky Duck* and you, too. Now Commander Donaldson's a fair officer.' He had looked hard at them, especially the bored-looking HO ratings. A few months before their lives had revolved around pubs, pictures and palais de danse and they were still civvies at heart. He had to turn them into matelots; it might with luck, save their young lives. 'But he'll come down like a ton of bricks on any sloppiness and dereliction of duty. So bear that in mind, you ratings. Do your best and he'll play ball with yer. Don't and you'll be on the rattle' – he meant a charge – 'before yer can say Jack Robinson. All right, lads,' he had said cheerfully, ''s the end of the prayer meeting. Dismiss.' Behind his back he had crossed his fingers for luck and hoped they'd take his advice.

CPO Tidmus was to be disappointed. At eight the following Monday morning Commander Donaldson did his first rounds of his new command. Followed at regulation distance by CPO Tidmus and Sub-Lieutenant Smythe, he set off, gleaming brass telescope under his right arm as if he were in charge of one of the new Prince of Wales-class battleships instead of a battered mine-sweeper first commissioned in World War

One.

He was in his best uniform, had not drunk more than two whiskies with his porridge and his lemon-yellow, haggard face looked a little healthy. Still, it was soon to become clear that his temper was as fierce as ever. Unlike most skippers he started in the ward-rooms and mess decks at the bottom of the *Black Swan* instead of on the deck; and, watching, CPO Tidmus, who had served under many captains, could see that his anger at what he saw was growing by the minute.

Together the three of them clattered down the metal ladder to the second of the mess decks, where the crew was waiting for them. Tidmus barked, 'Stand by yer bunks ... captain's inspection.'

The ratings clicked to attention, though Smythe, as afraid of the new skipper as presumably the crew were, didn't think they did so very smartly, but then he reasoned, he had three years of training at Dartmouth behind him. Donaldson touched his hand to his cap in salute and said, 'Please stand at ease.' Slowly he started to walk between the slung hammocks, past the metal tables that ran the length of the crew's quarters. Behind, Smythe's nose wrinkled at the stink, a mixture of oil, stale human sweat and the odour of damp bedding.

Donaldson paused abruptly. His gaze had fallen on the crew's unwashed tea mugs and tin plates, which still bore the traces of their breakfast, the usual bits of sausage and bacon rind, set in congealed grease now. In the centre of the unwashed table there was a great seven-pound issue tin of plum jam, its lid roughly opened by a tin opener and a spoon standing upright in the cheap sugary jam.

Tidmus saw the direction of the captain's gaze as he glared at the unsightly mess. Hastily he said, trying to defend the crew, 'The ratings don't have proper tools as yet, sir. So everybody digs in with his jackknife. That's why it looks a bit o' a lash-up.'

Strangely enough Donaldson accepted the hasty explanation, but he hadn't gone another pace when he spotted the half-eaten loaf of bread smeared with oily fingerprints lying in a pool of cold tea further on. 'They don't need tools, Chiefie, to muck that about, do they?' he asked pointedly. Donaldson didn't wait for the old petty officer's answer. Instead he said, 'No bread ration for breakfast tomorrow, Chiefie. Make a note of it. Tomorrow morning the cooks hand out dog biscuits.'

'Sir.' Tidmus snapped as the crew moaned. They knew the iron-hard dog biscuits already. They even had the name of the famous dog-food supplier printed across their surface: 'Spillers'.

They passed on into the evil-smelling 'heads', the walls of the latrines adorned with pornographic graffiti and the usual cheerful legend 'It's no use standing on the seat, the crabs in this place jump six feet.' Below there was another one, smeared in what Smythe could take only to be human ordure. It read: 'This bloody roundhouse is no good at all. The seat's too high and the hole's too small.'

Donaldson flushed angrily. 'Disgraceful!' he snorted. 'CPO, ensure that those heads are cleaned up immediately.'

'Sir.' Tidmus looked at Smythe and grimaced. It was a warning look. Now that Donaldson was on the warpath he found fault time and time again. The fire hoses weren't curled properly. The ammunition wasn't stacked close enough to the Oerlikon quick-firer. The sweeps were ready, but not for an instant launching as they should be ... On and on, again and again with Donaldson's normally yellow face flushed an angry crimson as if he might explode at any moment.

In the end the new captain did, when he came to examine the Carley floats, which were to be used if the order came to abandon ship. His experienced eye noted that the tins of provisions that would be used to keep shipwrecked crew members alive if they were forced to abandon ship were missing. He swung round and faced the old petty officer accusingly. 'Well,' he demanded, 'what do you make of that?'

Tidmus was perplexed. He knew instinctively that one of the crew, perhaps some hard-boiled three-striper, who would know about the Carley floats' tins of food, had nicked them one dark night and flogged them to the civvies on George Street's black market. The old sweats wouldn't stop at anything to get the money for more ale. 'Dockies,' he heard himself answering. 'They'd know about the grub. They've left us the water but the food they've nicked, the thieving bastards. Typical Hull dockie. We risk our necks and they nick our food. Bastards!'

Donaldson ignored the hurriedly dreamed-up explanation. 'Never mind the Hull dockies. Why weren't these missing items discovered earlier and replaced at once? We can be ordered to sea at any moment. Tidmus?'

Chiefie was caught off guard and Smythe felt for the old man with his false teeth and limp as he stuttered, 'Don't rightly know, sir. I'll see to it that there are regular inspections in the future, even if I do them mesen.'

Donaldson didn't seem satisfied with Tidmus's words. He swung round on Smythe, eyes angry, and the young sub-lieutenant realized then just how frightening the skipper could be. There was something more than the normal rage of the typical skipper who could wield total power over the crew on his ship. In Donaldson's case, he told himself at that moment, it was almost akin to madness. 'Smythe, I'm going to make you responsible for this matter. I can't have my petty officers bearing the brunt of duties of this nature. They have other duties to attend to. Is that understood?'

CPO Tidmus shot the young sub-lieutenant a sympathetic look. Smythe ignored it. He knew that if he was going to become a real officer he'd have to face up to Commander Donaldson, even if he were slightly crazy. The crew wouldn't respect him if he toadied to the captain. He wouldn't respect himself, either. 'Yessir,' he snapped back. 'I'll attend to the matter.'

'See that you do, Smythe.'

Donaldson turned now to an unhappy CPO Tidmus. 'All right, Chief Petty Officer, send the men to their stations. Ensure that each and every one of them is familiar with his duties. I want no more slackness on this ship. I'll crack down hard – very hard indeed – on anyone who doesn't meet my standards. That's it. Dismiss.'

Donaldson was true to his words. Despite his heavy drinking, he was here, there and everywhere during the long working hours that he now imposed upon his makeshift crew. Despite the rotten weather he kept the soft young HO men – mostly callow youths who had only seen the sea on bank holidays, unlike the three-stripers, who came from the coast – out in the bitter coastal rain squalls, which turned to sleet on most days. Now there were no hot mugs of steaming cocoa sent up by the cooks below at regular intervals. Nor were the fly spit-and-draws of sailors sheltering out of the icy wind that seemed to come straight from Siberia allowed any longer. Most skippers might have turned a blind eye to a man doing a four-hour watch in sub-zero temperatures having a quick clandestine puff at his issue Woodbine. Not Donaldson. He'd appear out of nowhere, followed by CPO Tidmus, notebook and pencil at the ready, crying angrily, 'Put that man on the rattle, Chief Petty Officer – smoking illegally while on duty.' And an ever reluctant Chiefie would do so, knowing that Donaldson was building up the crew's resentment against him; something that might well have adverse effects when it came to action.

Not that such matters worried Donaldson. Once when the CPO had attempted to broach the subject, as an intermediary between the lower deck and the captain, Donaldson had cut him short with a curt, 'I don't ask the men to love me, Chiefie. If they like they can fear me – hate me. It doesn't matter to me. What I want from them is that they *obey* me. No more and no less.'

Yet if the crew feared, perhaps indeed hated Commander Donaldson, they had to admit that he was a brave man. Two weeks after he had taken over the command of the *Black Swan* they were out just beyond Flamborough Head, practising mining drills, with their speed reduced to less than ten knots as they swept the rough seas beneath the majestic white cliffs of the Head, when a lookout sang out urgently, 'Enemy aircraft bearing—'

The rest of the young rating's words were cut by the harsh rat-tat-tat of machine-gun fire, as the Junkers 88 came sweeping in at zero feet, machine guns blazing. For a moment no one reacted – they were caught completely by surprise by the sudden attack, save for the captain. In one and the same movement he slid down from the bridge, grabbed the forrard Lewis gun and, swinging the heavy World War One machine gun round, started firing immediately.

All around him the enemy bullets slammed into the upper deck, splintering woodwork, bringing down the radio mast in a shower of blue angry sparks and shattering the glass of the bridge into a glittering spider's web of broken shards. The enemy fire didn't worry Donaldson one bit. As the two-engined fighter-bomber flashed overhead, dragging its evil shadow across the minesweeper, he swung the heavy gun round and peppered her blue belly with slugs. Almost immediately dark smoke started to stream from the Junkers' port engine. It started to cough and splutter and began to lose height at once. Still Donaldson continued firing, ignoring the German gunner halfway down the fuselage, his goggled face under the leather helmet clearly visible as he pumped bullets at the lone figure who had taken up the challenge, while CPO Tidmus yelled above the racket, 'Use your rifles, men! Give the skipper some support. Open fire, you gormless buggers.'

But Donaldson didn't need the support of Tidmus's 'gormless buggers'. He had already inflicted the fatal wound on the German plane. It came lower and lower, trailing its death wake of black behind it. It disappeared behind the cliff. Donaldson relaxed at his Lewis gun. The crew tensed expectantly. Next moment there it was. A muffled crash, the ear-splitting rending of tortured metal, followed an instant later by a burst of cherry-red flame.

Suddenly the crew were cheering and whooping, some of the ratings throwing their caps in the air with joy, others clapping and whistling through two fingers like they might at some peacetime football match when the home side was winning.

CPO Tidmus beamed at Smythe as the captain pulled down the barrel of the ugly-looking machine gun to say, 'All right, Chiefie, splice the mainbrace. I think the men deserve a wet.'

That increased the volume of the crew's cheering, and before CPO Tidmus went to see the keg of duty rum was brought on deck for the now happy ratings he whispered out of the side of his mouth to a smiling Smythe, 'I think the skipper's doing it, sir. He's getting the men on to his side. I do hope so.'

Then he was gone, leaving the young sub-lieutenant to wonder at the strange workings of the ship's crew. Hate turning into admiration at the cost of a couple of Jerries' lives, burned to death in the blazing Junkers. He shook his head in mock bewilderment. He would write to Mummy about today's events, especially the shooting down of the Jerry plane, but he suspected she would not be able to understand them even if she lived to be a hundred, the poor dear.

Six

He knew he'd struck lucky as soon as the other civilian in the flashy jacket and baggy un-English trousers opened his mouth. 'Say, buddy,' he said, 'where does a guy get some grub, a cold beer and some action around this goddam dump?'

'An American!' The startling thought flashed through Paddy Kerrigan's mind immediately as he recognized the accent. It was the Americans, a rarity in Hull, whom he had been taught to look out for by his instructor in Hamburg. As Dr Ransau, if that was his real name, had warned him more than once in those last days of training at Hamburg's Hotel Phoenix, 'We know the *Amis* are going to make the attempt. What we don't know, Kerrigan, is *when*. It's your job in Hull to find that out for us.' Was this his chance to do so?

He didn't give himself a chance to consider the matter, as the Yank brushed close to him in the passage that led to the dingy pub not far from the old German Seamen's Mission. Instead, he said, feeling his shoulders begin to ache again from a day carrying a hod full of bricks up and down a ladder at the building site on Hedon Road, 'Sure I can show you some action, me fine boyo.'

The Yank must have recognized his accent, too, for he said enthusiastically, 'Say, you're Irish, aren't you? Not one of these limey sons of bitches.'

'I am that.'

'Well, put it there.' The Yank thrust out his right hand. 'I'm from Boston, matey. My old mom came from the Old Country, God rest her soul. She was allus proud to be from the Old Sod.'

Paddy didn't know exactly what the 'Old Sod' was, but he supposed it was something to do with Ireland and said, 'And so she should. Now then, let's get ye some grub first.'

'None of that limey fart food,' the American protested hastily. 'I've had enough of that cabbage and those Brussels sprouts to last me a lifetime.'

'No, real English food. Put lead in yer pencil.'

Now it was the turn of his new-found

American friend to look puzzled by a new word. All the same he said enthusiastically, 'Lead on, matey. I'm goddam starving.'

They pushed their way underneath the heavy felt blackout curtain into the crowded warm fug of the fish and chip shop. It was full of poorly dressed civilians, mostly women, some wearing men's boots and caps, and drunken happy sailors, flushed and wearing their caps at the back of their heads, adding to the steam and smoke of the frying fish bubbling away in the pan of red-hot brown lard with the fumes from their cheap Woodbines.

Next to the heavy-bosomed woman, face dripping with sweat, another much younger one was cutting up newspaper into squares ready for the fish and chips, cigarette stuck to her bottom lip, telling anyone who wanted to listen just how good her 'Jack', presumably her husband, was. 'Knocker-up in t'morning has him up at seven and off to the docks. Twelve-hour shift and fixes his own supper. Never see him 'cept in bed,' and she would wink at the nearest sailor encouragingly, as if the last statement meant something of significance.

Once she looked at the Yank, but he didn't seem interested. Nor did Paddy Kerrigan, who watched hungrily as the chips in the bubbling dripping began to turn deep brown and crisp, the little bits of potato being propelled back and forth by the terrific heat as if they had a life of their own. He had a hard shift behind him, up and down the ladder with the hod over his right shoulder and another six bricks balanced upon a ring of old silk stocking on his head, all for fifteen bob. But it was worth it if he could scoff a large portion of those delightful chips.

'Next please,' the woman cutting the paper called, ready to wrap the order. Obediently the queue shuffled forward and suddenly Kerrigan felt the Yank press up against his backside and there was no mistaking the gesture and what it signified. The Yank had an erection!

Not one of them – a frigging nancy boy, he cursed to himself. Aloud he said, knowing that he had a vitally important contact with him, 'Do you fancy a double portion o' chips? I'm paying.'

'Chips?'

'Fried taties.'

'You mean french fries?'

'Come on, lads. Make up your mind,' the woman with the paragon of a husband urged. 'We ain't got all night. Old Jerry'll be dropping in soon for his one and each.'

That caused a laugh and hastily Kerrigan did his ordering, reaching for the vinegar and salt on the dirty counter, while the Yank, seemingly innocently, pressed himself harder against him.

Outside they felt the cold immediately, the steam from the paper parcel containing their fish and chips rising up and wreathing their faces in the light of what the locals called a 'bombers' moon', a half sphere of bright silver light.

'What do we do?' the Yank asked, puzzled, staring down at the open parcel. 'We ain't got nuthin' to eat them with.'

'Fingers were invented before forks,' Kerrigan answered, levering himself away from the Yank, eager to get at the chips while they were still hot and crisp. Inside the shop the cook was shouting above the roar of the extractor fan, 'No more fish, lads and lassies. Sorry, but we've run out.'

'Fucking Churchill,' an old man quavered. 'Can't even fucking well feed us. But then he never did do owt for the workers.'

'Over there,' Kerrigan suggested. 'In the door of that air-raid shelter. Be out of the wind there.'

The Yank accepted the suggestion with alacrity. Kerrigan knew why. The Yank was more interested in sex than fish and chips. The air-raid shelter would provide the ideal place for what the nancy boy had in mind, the dirty pervert.

Kerrigan took his time with the food. He wanted to get to know as much as possible before the other man got up to his nasty tricks. Then he'd have to turn tough. He wasn't interested in that kind of nasty sex. It was unnatural anyway, wasn't it?

He breathed hard over a hot piece of fish that burned his fingers, as cold as they were. 'How come you ended up here, pal?' he asked with seeming casualness. 'I thought you Yanks sailed into Liverpool.'

The Yank swallowed the hot chip he was eating and said, 'We do. But I got bored with Liverpool. No real action, if you follow my meaning, matey.' In the spectral silver light of the half moon, Kerrigan saw the look in the other man's eyes and recognized it for what it was. Now he was supposed to ask what 'real action' the Yank meant. But then he already knew what the frigging American pervert was after. So instead he asked, 'But why come to Hull, especially as your skipper might think you've jumped ship – and I suppose that could mean trouble for you in wartime.'

The Yank shook his head. 'Not him. His majesty's drunk half the time, that is when he's not after the arses of the cabin boys, if you get my meaning.'

Paddy Kerrigan pretended he didn't and the Yank went on with, 'Anyway, we're sailing for Hull here as soon as the convoy from New York is assembled.'

'In New York?'

'Nah, in Liverpool. Then we sail for Hull under the protection of the British frigging Royal frigging Navy.' He bit into his fried fish, as if in disgust. 'God only knows why we can't use our own boys from the US Navy. They're real seamen.' He broke off and, wrapping up the parcel of the remaining fish and chips, he threw it into the corner of the smelly air-raid shelter. 'Say, buddy, what about a little action now, eh? We don't want to spend the night shooting the breeze, do we? It's getting frigging cold –' he shuddered dramatically – 'and I don't want to get too cold.' He grabbed the front of his baggy pants to demonstrate exactly what he meant.

Paddy Kerrigan knew time was running out. He'd have to make a break with the nancy boy in a minute. All the same, he wanted to get as much information out of him as he could. 'Have you got a date for when your mates from Liverpool will arrive here in Hull?'

By the light of the moon, Kerrigan saw the sudden look of suspicion in the American's eyes. He knew at once he had gone too far.

The Yank looked at him hard and then said slowly, 'Say, buddy, why are you asking all them goddam questions? I thought you was after something else, buying me the grub and all. I thought you was one of us.' He moved forward threateningly, his desire vanished now.

'One of you?' Kerrigan parried desperately. 'I don't get you. Do you mean Irish – from the Old Country?'

'No, I don't frigging mean that,' the other man snarled. 'I mean you seem a bit too interested in the movement of our shipping. What are you, some kind of spy or something—' He stopped short, as if it had suddenly dawned upon him that he had hit the nail on the head. 'Jesus H. Christ,' he exclaimed excitedly, 'you *are* a goddam spy!'

'Now hang on', Kerrigan began, but already the Yank was drawing out a long seaman's knife which he had kept concealed underneath his overlong sweater.

'Brother,' the Yank breathed, stepping forward another pace, 'you really had me fooled. Fell for it hook, line and sinker. You ain't no Irish faggot, you're a goddam Kraut spy!'

'I'm no such thing.' Kerrigan dodged swiftly, twisting his hips like a professional ballet dancer as the Yank lunged at his guts. Next moment he grabbed at the other man's knife hand and yelped with pain as the sharp blade sliced through his fingers.

The Yank laughed crazily. 'That hurt, you spying bastard, didn't it? Now try this on for fucking size.' He lunged again as Paddy Kerrigan withdrew his bleeding fingers, gasping with pain and shock at the sudden attack, knowing at the same time that if he didn't do something the Yank would kill him. There was no doubt about that.

Instinctively he brought up his right knee. It caught the Yank between the legs just as he was about to thrust again.

The Yank gasped. His mouth fell open and vomit spurted out. Still he didn't relinquish hold of that killing knife. Paddy Kerrigan knew that this was his last chance. If he didn't finish the pansy boy off now, he wouldn't get a second chance. He smashed his heavy navvy's boot against the other man's shin. The Yank howled with pain and doubled up. Kerrigan didn't give him another chance. He brought his doubled fists, clubbed together, down on the nape of the American's neck. The killing knife clattered to the floor of the air-raid shelter as the sirens began to sound their dread warning, indicating the Jerries were coming back for their 'one of each'.

They alerted Kerrigan to the new danger. Soon the civvies would be tumbling out of their pubs and other dives for these overhead shelters. He had to deal with the Yank, now on his knees, gasping hoarsely for breath like a boxer refusing to go down for the count. He grabbed the knife, swung behind the American and pulled at his greasy long hair so that his head was forced back to reveal his skinny throat. He didn't hesitate as outside the flak started to thunder and the first German bombs screeched down with a frightening, banshee-like howl. Carefully, like a skilled barber intent on giving some favoured customer a good shave, he began to draw the blade across the faggot's throat.

Book Two

The Yanks Are Coming

One

The English Lords' signal was faint but definite. The huge listening towers of the German Navy picked it up immediately. Below in the concrete bomb-proof bunkers the bespectacled officers of the *Kriegsmarine*'s decoding service, products of US Ivy league colleges and Oxbridge, started to work on the British Admiralty code at once, while at his HQ Admiral Doenitz, the rat-faced head of the German submarine wolf-packs, waited impatiently for the first decodes.

The clever young officers knew the situation. The rumour about the first *Ami* convoy to Russia had been floating around the key decoding centres at Flensburg and Hamburg for weeks. Now it looked as if the final decision had been made in Washington and London. Doenitz, who hated perfidious Albion with a passion (he had been a prisoner of the English in World War One and lost his son and son-in-law in battle with them in this war), was already sneering, 'Now the Tommies will be fighting to the last American.'

Within thirty minutes flat, the languid young decoders with their clever faces and bored air, handkerchiefs tucked up their sleeves in the slightly decadent English fashion, had produced the first decodes. Immediately the teleprinters began clattering, dispatching the English plans to Admiral Doenitz's battle headquarters at Brest on the French coast.

Doenitz read them with pleasure. It was what he had been expecting all along. The American tankers and supply ships, carrying tanks, guns and food for the hard-pressed Russians, would now sail from Liverpool and assemble in the Humber off Hull ready for the long run to Murmansk. Once out in the North Sea the English would take over the protection of this first *Ami* convoy.

Doenitz gave one of his wolfish smiles at the thought. What protection could the Tommies offer against the whole might of the German U-Boat and the Luftwaffe as they ploughed steadily northwards at the speed of the slowest vessel in the convoy, which he calculated couldn't be more than eight knots?

Still holding the first decodes in his skeletal hand, he turned to his adjutant and rasped in the harsh Prussian accent of his, 'Dietz, see if you can get me an urgent connection to the Führer HQ. Tell them that this is a matter of the most vital importance. The Führer must know of it at once. *Klar?*'

'*Klar, Herr Grossadmiral!*'

Surprisingly enough Doenitz received the order to scramble within the hour. Now he sat expectantly at the phone waiting for the Führer to speak. Of old he knew the Führer showed little interest in the navy; indeed, when Hitler was forced to launch new ships for the *Kriegsmarine*, he was invariably seasick even when they were still in the harbour. Perhaps that had something to do with it. The army really was the apple of his eye. Still, what he was now about to propose to the leader would affect the army fighting for its very life in the snowy wastes of Russia and perhaps even affect the new 'special relationship', as Churchill called it, between America and England. He firmly believed it would.

'Doenitz?' There was no mistaking that voice. It was that of the Führer.

Doenitz sat to attention, such was the effect of his being in the Führer's presence, even if it was only over the telephone wire. '*Heil, mein Führer*,' he barked back, half raising his right arm in salute until he realized that Hitler wouldn't be able to see him.

'*Na*. Doenitz.' Hitler lowered his voice and suddenly seemed to be in an almost jovial mood. '*Wo brennsts*? Where's the fire?'

'I hope, if you will forgive the crudity, *mein Führer*, under the arses of that sod Churchill and his admirals.'

Hitler laughed shortly. 'Tell me, Doenitz.'

'Well, as you know, *mein Führer*, the English and the Americans are geting together at last, now that that Jew Roosevelt has taken them into a war here in Europe that is no concern of theirs. It would help if we could shake this supposed new friendship between the Anglo-Saxon countries.'

Hitler cleared his throat. 'I don't like my soldiers playing politics, as you know, Doenitz, but pray tell me more.'

Swiftly and expertly Doenitz sketched in his attack plan for the first American convoy to be sent to help the beleaguered Russians, which, as he said, 'will take the pressure off our brave fellows in Russia'. He added, 'But there could be more to it than that, *mein Führer.'*

'How?'

'In this manner, sir. Last summer, so I have read, sixty per cent of Americans stated they didn't trust the English. They were arch-imperialists, who had only the preservation of their empire and their political interests at heart. They maintained that Americans were being used as England's dupes.'

From the way that Hitler allowed him to talk so long, Doenitz felt he had captured the Führer's interest. So he continued. 'Well, sir, if that's the feeling of the average American, we can do something with this American convoy that will fuel their anti-English mood.'

'How?'

'The convoy will be protected by the English Royal Navy solely. No *Ami* warship will take part in it. If the Royal Navy fails to protect the American merchantmen, then it could be that—'

Hitler beat him to it. 'That the Americans will feel the arrogant English have let them down, eh, Doenitz?'

'Exactly, sir.' Doenitz mopped his damp brow. He always sweated when he had to deal with the Führer on this one-to-one basis.

'*Eine kapitale Idee*,' the Führer gushed. As always he had begun to believe that the idea stemmed from him. 'I shall alert Air Fleet Six in Holland, the Seventh in Norway. Goering will take care of the details. They must be brought up to maximum strength at once and placed on permanent red alert till this American convoy sails. You, my dear fellow, I don't need to give orders to.'

Doenitz's drawn, haggard face cracked into a wintry smile. The Führer was not often given to praise. Suddenly he felt very pleased with himself, as Hitler concluded with, 'You shall plan the U-boat campaign against the convoy in any way you wish, Doenitz. I ask you one thing only, sink as many of those damned ships as you can. *Ende.*'

The red scrambler phone went dead in Doenitz's hand. For a moment he simply sat there as if mesmerized, bathing in the warm glow of the Führer's praise. He had the Führer's approval for a max effort attack. Now he'd show Fat Hermann, the roly-poly head of the Luftwaffe, Herman Goering, and all the rest of those 'monocle Fritzes' of the general staff what the German navy could really do. For too long in this war they had maligned the navy, maintaining it should be virtually closed down and its sailors be sent to the Russian front as infantrymen, instead of idling in port drinking too much and chasing loose women. He beamed. Karl Doenitz looked at his haggard face in the mirror opposite and swore aloud, 'It's going to be a massacre, my dear Mr Churchill...'

On the other side of the Channel, in his office in 10 Downing Street, Churchill, too, sat alone, staring reflectively at his image in the window oppposite. The British Prime Minister might have possessed many gifts, but not that of second sight. He knew nothing of what Admiral Doenitz, the commander of the deadly U-boat wolf packs, had in store for him at that particular moment. All the same, he was worried.

He knew, as Doenitz did, unknown to him, just how fragile the new Anglo-American 'special relationship', as he called it, was. It had taken him nearly two years to bring it about and he knew that it could fall disastrously apart in a matter of a mere two days if things went wrong in the North Sea. After all, it was only a matter of twenty years ago that leading American politicians and military had called for a war with Britain. Even now there were the American Firsters, like Colonel Lindbergh, who still agitated against Americans fighting 'England's wars'.

The premier sucked his ugly false teeth and then looked as an afterthought at the glass of brandy he always kept ready on his desk. So far everything seemed to be going right with the 'American convoy ploy', as his new-found friend President Roosevelt called it. But he knew Roosevelt. It was said of him that he played his cards so close to his chest that the print wiped off on his shirt. In reality he couldn't really trust the president, who was crippled and bound to his wheelchair. If anything went wrong with this common venture, Roosevelt would disown the 'special relationship' and let himself be led by US public opinion. Sadly, as he had learned from his long years in politics, American presidents always felt that international considerations came second to the sordid business of their winning the next presidential election. Thoughtfully he reached out and took a careful sip at the glass of brandy. Security had already reported some minor problems with the secret convoy at Hull in remotest Yorkshire. He knew little about the port save for that old sailors, saying, 'From Hull, Halifax and high water may the good Lord preserve us.' It seemed an apt saying at this particular moment, Churchill told himself. Every precaution, however minor, had to be taken to ensure the US convoy sailed from Hull and reached Murmansk in sufficient numbers to make the business seem worthwhile to Roosevelt and his service chiefs, plus the Great American Public. After all, the whole great country lived and thrived on the lies of the publicity-mongers. Churchill thought it had something to do with the power of advertising over the American man in the street.

He dismissed the idle thought and concentrated on the task at hand. The mission must succeed in part, sufficiently to make the Americans believe that helping the Russians was worthwhile. Yet at the same time there had to be losses in order to convince Roosevelt and his service chiefs that an invasion of Europe was not feasible this year of 1942. The ship losses he anticipated once the convoy came up against the Germans on the continent should make that clear to them, he hoped.

Churchill sighed. Life at the top was complicated, he told himself. With a flourish, he drained his glass and then, with his fountain pen, he scrawled on the single sheet of paper that his aides would forward to those in charge of security at that remote East Yorkshire port:

ACTION THIS DAY! Have noted security problems. Pray clear up same PDQ. Be ruthless. The special relationship between the two Anglo-Saxon peoples is at stake. Winston Spencer Churchill.

Two

Paddy Kerrigan had had a hard day on the building site. The foreman bricklayer had picked on him again, shouting, 'Ruddy lazy Mick,' chasing him up and down the ladder with his heavy hod and the bricks balanced on his head until he'd been about to throw down the bloody hod and slap the Yorkshire bastard. He'd kept his temper, though, and now, sweaty and stinking of cement, he would have dearly loved a bath. But in the Kilmartin boarding house a bath – 'only nine inches of water, mate, remember' – cost a ruddy shilling, and for a bob he could buy a jug of ale at the nearby Sailor's Return pub.

Besides, the Irishman didn't have the energy to light the boiler, forage enough wood from the bomb-damaged houses all around for fuel and then beg Kilmartin – the mean Ulster bastard – for half a bucket of slack and coal to keep the boiler going. It would be all too much of a chore. He would concentrate on sending his message to Hamburg, which would bring a discreet package of crisp new five-pound notes from the *Abwehr*'s contact in the supposed neutral Swiss Embassy in London

Flexing his stiff muscles and attempting to slake his thirst with water from the single tap at the sink, he set about preparing the transmitter, slinging the wire over a gap in the plaster above his head and taking the little high-power radio from its case. In minutes he was ready – he'd trained often enough on the apparatus back in Hamburg. Cautious as ever, he cracked his knuckles, trying to bring back flexibility to his work-stiffened fingers, and stared about the dingy little bedroom. Everything seemed in order. Outside all was quiet. The dockies on the night shift had already gone to work and it was too early for the pubs to be open, and down below the Kilmartin brood would undoubtedly be sitting around a roaring coal fire listening to the English propaganda on the radio, though at nine o'clock they turned religiously to 'Radio Bremen' to listen to that snarling supercilious Lord Haw-Haw. It wasn't that the Kilmartins were interested in the vitriol poured out by that renegade Irishman with his posh English voice. All they wanted to hear from him was whether Hull was about to be bombed that night. Everyone in England knew that the propagandist in the pay of the Germans could be relied on to give a true account of the Luftwaffe's bombing of their country.

Ready now, Kerrigan poised with his work-stiff, dirty finger above the morse key. He was not an imaginative man, nor one given to unreasoning fears. All the same, he knew that every time he pressed the key he was putting his life on the line. Transmit a second or two too long and the English location-detection devices, which were everywhere these days, as he knew, and the law would be on his trail in a flash. As usual he gabbled off a quick Hail Mary, as if he were back with the nuns in Ireland, and started to transmit...

The *Abwehr* had spoiled him once they had signed him up as an agent officially. There had been parties in the best hotels, the Atlantic and the Vierjahreszeiten and the like, as many high-class whores as he could manage and promises, promises, promises all the time. Kerrigan had not allowed his head to be turned much by the *Abwehr*'s generosity. Always he remembered his dead father, murdered by those English swine of the Black and Tans, and the holy cause of a free Ireland. He had worked hard for the *Abwehr* because he wanted to show them he wasn't the usual happy-go-lucky Mick who lived for the day and drank too much. He was dead serious and they seemed to acknowledge that, for German money and arms had begun to flow into Southern Ireland as they had done in the First World War. But now the Germans didn't want the Irish to rise and throw the English into the Irish Sea. Instead, being more realistic than their imperial German predecessors, they wanted to know the details of the English armaments industry, her coastal defences, the location of the new RAF airfields, which were going up everywhere after Munich – anything that might be of use to the Third

Reich in the war.

After a while Kerrigan had begun to realize that he was working more for the *Abwehr* than he was for the boyos and the Movement. In reality he was a German spy, there was no other description for his activities. All the same, he knew, too, that as long as he hurt the English under German command he was helping to free dear old Ireland from the English yoke. Still, there was his own future to be considered, too.

In early 1942 he had been summoned to the Hotel Vierjahreszeiten on Hamburg's internal lake to be greeted by no less a person than old Father Christmas, the white-haired, benevolent-looking head of the *Abwehr*. In real life the sloppily dressed civilian with his twin dachshunds that he adored more than his own daughters was an admiral in the German navy. Now that Kerrigan had been presented to the mysterious spymaster, however, he could hardly believe it. Admiral Canaris looked anything but a high-ranking officer, with his stoop, grubby, unpressed clothes and somewhat affected, even effeminate manner.

He greeted Kerrigan effusively, and then started discussing the *Abwehr*'s next mission for him in a decidedly realistic businesslike manner. Stroking one of his ugly, fat-bellied dachshunds, he said, 'We're sending you to England. I know it's very risky, my dear Kerrigan, but we will do our utmost to ensure that nothing happens to you. In the final analysis, if things go wrong, our friends – bought friends, it is understand – and in that little country money can buy anything,' he added with a malicious smile. 'In Switzerland, that is. At all events, the people at the Swiss Legation will look after you. Now, what is it we want to do?'

Rapidly Canaris had explained the business with the first American convoy to Russia, while Kerrigan had listened intently. When the spymaster was finished, and while the fat dachshund had waddled off to urinate in the corner under his master's benign gaze, Kerrigan had exclaimed, 'But I'll be taking a tremendous risk, Herr Admiral!'

'I know, Kerrigan,' Canaris had agreed easily. 'But we're going to make it worthwhile for you.'

'How, sir?'

In this way. This will be your last mission for the *Abwehr*. Once I was in this very risky business myself,' he smiled fondly at the other man, 'and my luck ran out. I was in the condemned cell. I had to kill a priest to escape. I know the problems, Kerrigan.'

Kerrigan looked at the smiling spymaster aghast. That harmless-looking man with his white hair, benevolent look and silly dogs had actually killed a holy priest. It didn't seem possible. For a couple of moments he couldn't speak he was so shocked.

'Sooner or later your luck will run out too, Kerrigan. We value you too highly to let that happen. We shall pull you out of this deadly game before then.'

'How, sir?'

Again Canaris smiled. 'In the same manner that most of my colleagues are secretly preparing for the inevitable.'

Kerrigan didn't know exactly what the 'inevitable' was, but he guessed Canaris meant Germany's defeat. He didn't rise to the bait, but continued to listen in silence.

'We shall provide you with a new identity and a new life, plus enough in the way of funds to keep you for many years until you have established yourself.'

'And Ireland?' he had asked after what had seemed a long silence.

'Ireland.' Canaris seemed to toy with the word, as if it were totally new to him. 'Ireland ... What can one do about that benighted coutry, I wonder? Kerrigan had flushed, but then he had realized that Canaris was giving the matter serious consideration and he had relaxed. 'I am much older than you, my dear Karrigan,' Canaris said, 'and I have known of the problem with Ireland for a long time. The conflict there has gone on for many years and many people, good and bad, have died trying to solve it. Without success. Perhaps there is no solution to the problem of the Irish.' He had laughed softly. 'Perhaps like the Jews the Irish must be spread across the globe, though I don't know about the Irish. At least the Jews make money.' His voice had risen. 'So, my dear Kerrigan, my advice to you is to carry out this mission, take what our government will give you in the way of money and a new identity and disappear into a happy life rather than this one of constant hate and strife...'

Now, as he prepared to transmit, his revolver as usual lying on the table next to him, as regulations demanded, Kerrigan remembered Canaris's last words to him. He nodded his head. Perhaps the old fox of a spymaster was right. There was no future for Ireland – or for people like him, devoting their lives to what appeared to be a lost cause. The time had perhaps come to chuck it in and start anew.

He gripped the key more firmly and sent his call sign, his mind only half on the job at hand. 'Yank ships arriving forty-eight hours' time, Hull.' He tapped out the vital information. '*Anticipate six tankers, ten merchantmen, two ammo ships*—'

Outside he heard a slight noise that disturbed him somehow. He increased his speed. He had to get the transmission over and his set hidden away. 'Report Yank ships to stay in Humber—'

He stopped dead. There was no mistaking Kilmartin's ugly Ulster accent, as he whispered, 'The Paddy's up there, top room to the right, sir.' The alarming thought shot through his mind. The Ulster bastard was shopping him to the law. His hand fell from the brass key as if it were red hot. What was he to do?

He had rehearsed this moment in his mind time and time again through his sleepless nights. He had thought he had it all worked out. Now he seemed mesmerized, unable to act. Someone was squeaking his way up the bomb-damaged stairs and he knew it wasn't Kilmartin. Like all Ulsterman the landlord of the boarding house was a noisy bugger. No, this was someone else who meant no good.

Abruptly he became aware of the danger of his position. He grabbed for the revolver, his message forgotten. Suddenly his nerves were jingling electrically as the adrenaline surged through his bloodstream. He was in trouble. Carefully he eased off the revolver's safety catch as he prepared for the worst.

Another squeak and a muffled curse. It was the loose floorboard just outside his door. Carefully he rose to his feet. Should he fire through the door? It was made of plywood. The bullet would badly hurt anyone standing there even after having passed through the thin wood. He decided against it. He must not give his hand away yet.

The moments ticked away leadenly. He wet his suddenly dry lips. Was whoever was behind that door never going to act? Then it happened. A heavy shoulder leaned against the wood and the handle of the door began to turn slowly. Nothing. The door was locked and he had wedged the usual chair underneath the knob.

Outside the unknown man cursed softly once more. From below he heard Kilmartin say something, which he couldn't make out. He pulled the hammer of the revolver back softly. If the unknown man was serious he was going to attempt to break that door down in half a mo, he told himself.

Next instant Kerrigan was proved right. The heavy shoulder crashed against the door with full force. The frail lock splintered. The chair flew back and a heavy-set middle-aged man in a blue serge suit and wearing a trilby staggered into the room. He took in the scene immediately. The naked electric bulb, the wire running to the ceiling, the transmitter and the skinny man standing there in his dirty, cement-stained clothes, bearing a heavy revolver in his hand.

In his turn Kerrigan recognized the civilian for what he was: a middle-aged rozzer, who was too old to have been called up for the forces, and he was unarmed. But at that moment, with his imagination running wild, knowing that this could be the end of the road for him, he saw the lone unarmed civilian as just another Black and Tan, like the men who had killed his dear old dad so long ago.

'Give me that weapon,' the man said in his slow East Yorkshire accent. 'Come on, let's be having it. We don't want no trouble, do we, son?' He took a step forward, right hand outstretched, as if he were in complete charge of the situation. He even managed a wary smile.

'Stop there!' Kerrigan commanded, mind in a whirl.

'Now don't be daft, lad. You 'aven't got a chance. Give me that popgun and there'll be no trouble. I'll see you'll get a fair crack o' the whip.' He hesitated and then took another step forward.

Kerrigan didn't hesitate. The middle-aged Black and Tan was just like the rest of the killing murderous bastards. They thought they could do everything. His finger took first pressure on the trigger. The civilian saw the whitening of his knuckle and knew he was in danger. 'Now that's enough,' he ordered. 'Put that re—'

Kerrigan fired. The bullet caught the other man in the stomach. His guts seemed to explode in a flurry of blood and a red gorge of shattered flesh. 'Oh Christ,' he moaned, his false teeth slipping out of his gaping mouth with the shock of that terrible blow. With his right hand still outstretched for the revolver, he sank slowly to his knees. His head dropped almost sadly. Next moment he collapsed in a dying heap.

From outside there came the sound of angry shouts. Whistles shrilled. Someone yelled orders. Kilmartin shouted. Heavy boots started to pound up the stairs. For a moment Kerrigan panicked. He threw a wild glance around him, looking for a way out. There seemed none. Then he had it.

Stuffing his revolver into his thick leather belt that all hod carriers wore to prevent being ruptured under the weight of the bricks they carried, he reached up and easily pulled himself to the ceiling. Hanging there, he butted his head against the weakened lathes. They cracked immediately, giving him a hole big enough to crawl through. A moment later he was crouched on the wet tiles, blinking abruptly in the sudden darkness.

He was used to heights; still, the tiles were wet and slippery. Carefully he rose and, balancing himself with his hands outstretched, he tottered to the edge of the roof. His plan was to use it to swing into the next house, a bomb ruin. With a bit of luck he'd beat the rozzers and be off. He'd work his way down to London and there the money-greedy 'neutral' Swiss would see him all right just as 'Father Christmas' had promised him they would back in Hamburg.

But that wasn't to be. As he balanced there, letting his eyes become accustomed to the darkness, he was caught in light with alarming suddenness, and a harsh authoritarian voice demanded, 'Stop there! We've got you!'

All hope seeped from Kerrigan's body, as if someone had opened a tap. He'd had it; there was no hope for him.

Three

Together with CPO Tidmus, Smythe watched as the ratings of the *Black Swan* jostled and joked with each other as they lined up with their mess tins and pannikans in front of the big oaken keg bearing the legend, '*The King, God Bless Him*'. They were waiting expectantly for their daily issue of rum and water – their grog. Opposite, Commander Donaldson watched too, a gloomy look on his dour drunkard's face.

'The skipper's not looking at his best, Chiefie,' Smythe ventured, knowing that he had found a friend in the old petty officer and that he could speak freely to him.

'Well, sir, it's about time for the Captain's Requestmen to start, once the lads have had their grog, and Commander Donaldson hates Captain Requestmen sessions with a passion.

'Captain Requestmen?' Smythe queried.

'Like the CO's orderly room in the Royal Marines, sir,' Tidmus answered, keeping a wary eye on the happy matelots. 'The ratings see the captain and put in their requests. Hence the name.'

'I see,' Smythe said as the petty officer acting as purser started to dish out the rum, which by regulation was to be drunk on the spot, especially when in port. That way the navy thought it would stop drunkenness, but as Tidmus commented, 'There's no way of preventing sippers, sir.'

Smythe gave a mock groan. 'I don't think I'll ever learn all this naval lingo. What in the name of God is sippers?'

'Oh, if a rating owes another matelot something, he might pay if off with a sip of his daily rum ration. That's sippers.'

In a matter of minutes the rum issue was over, accompanied with suddenly flushed cheeks and an outbreak of coughing among the young HO men, who weren't yet used to the powerful rum. Now Donaldson straightened up and nodded to CPO Tidmus. 'All right, Chief Petty Officer, I'm ready for

Captain's Requestmen. Make it snappy. I'm expecting something.' He jerked his head in the direction of the Humber.

CPO Tidmus snapped to attention, pulled out his notebook and barked, 'Just one, sir. Able Seaman Thompson.'

'What's he want, Chief Petty Officer?'

'Permission to grow a beard, sir.'

'Does he know that once he gets permission to grow, he can't use a razor without my permission for three months? I don't want dirty sailors asking for permission to grow a beard as a dodge not to shave and stay dirty.'

'Yes, sir. I've told him.'

'All right, wheel him up.'

Thompson, a pasty-faced sailor with surprisingly large buttocks, came forward, cap neatly under his right arm. A matelot, perhaps a little tight from the rum, whistled softly. Tidmus knew why. Behind his back the other ratings called Thompson 'Gladys' and made simpering gestures. Tidmus guessed that was why he wanted to grow a beard, to prove his masculinity.

Donaldson looked the pasty-faced sailor up and down and it was clear that he didn't particularly like what he saw. Finally he said, 'All right, you know the rules, Thompson. Permission granted.' Smartly the sailor turned round, a grin on his pudgy face, while one of the crowd of ratings kissed the back of his hand with a loud sucking noise and whispered, 'Kiss me quick, me mother's drunk.'

Tidmus frowned severely, but before he could remonstrate with the offending rating a much older sailor, one of the ancient three stripers, called angrily, 'Permission to have a grudge fight, Chiefie.'

'What?' Tidmus asked, startled by the un-regulation interruption. 'What did you say, Higgins?'

''Tis that bugger of a cockney, Hawkins, sir. I want a grudge fight. He bloody well pinched the end of me banger and it was a NAAFI banger, not one of them pusser's ones. I bought it with my own money at the NAAFI.'

'What the devil's name is going on there, Chief Petty Officer?' Donaldson broke in angrily. 'Who's talking in the ranks while on parade, I say?'

CPO Tidmus's old wrinkled face flushed. 'It's Leading Hand Higgins, sir. He says he wants a grudge fight with Hawkins, sir. He says Hawkins has pinched, er, stolen his sausage and he wants his revenge.'

Donaldson puffed out his chest, as if he

might explode at any moment. But the explosion that everyone now expected never came, for before the captain could let off steam loud music came suddenly from the estuary, echoing back and forth metallically from one bank to the other of the Humber. In a flash all eyes turned to the river and there they saw the long, slow tanker, a huge Stars & Stripes painted on its hull, its loudspeakers blasting out that tune that most of the old hands remembered well from the Great War. *'The Yanks are coming ... So prepare, say a prayer ... For the Yanks are coming ... over ... over there...'*

Behind it came an even larger merchantman, its decks crowded with aeroplane fuselages and huge crates carrying the wings belonging to the fighters. Its loudspeakers, too, were going full blast. This time the tune was unfamiliar to the gaping British sailors, something about the 'Yellow Rose of Texas', whatever that was. But there was no mistaking the fact this vessel was American also. CPO Tidmus sighed to Sub-Lieutenant Smythe as if he couldn't really believe the evidence of his own eyes. 'Hellfire, sir, the bloody Yanks have arrived in full frigging force...'

And they had. That night the bars, hotels,

pubs and dives of the north-east seaport were packed with noisy Americans of all shades and colours: white, off-white, black, yellow and in a couple of instances what seemed a dull pink. They were totally unlike British merchant seamen in their dull shabby overalls and dungarees. These Yanks wore flamboyant clothes, smoked cigars, shouted at each other at the tops of their voices across the bars and tossed pound notes on to the counters for drinks that might have cost a couple of shillings at the most, crying to the flustered barmaids, 'Take it outa that funny money, honey, and keep the change.'

No woman was safe from them, it seemed, even when she was with another man. Whore or simple housewife enjoying a shandy, the Americans would approach them, holding out gifts of precious, almost unheard of nylons as if they were offering fake pearls to some gullible native. Not that the women minded. The Yanks were too generous in comparison even to a British merchant seaman, who had just completed a voyage and had a pocket full of a month's pay.

Naturally, by the time it was approaching closing time – 'Closing time, what the hell d'ya mean? I've just started drinking, buddy' – fighting had broken out among the British and the Americans. In various states of drunkenness, the would-be combatants were thrust out into the chilly blackout to continue their battle there; and even the most experienced British merchant seaman was surprised when the white Yanks pulled knives on them. 'That's not fair,' they'd protest drunkenly. 'You can expect that sort of a caper from yer darkies and chinks, but not from white men.'

By midnight the hard-pressed local police were summoning reinforcements from towns all about Hull – Beverly, Grimsby, Goole and the like. The brawls and the fights were getting out of hand and the local dock-yard bobbies, who were used to seamen's brawls, didn't really know how to tackle these Yanks, who wouldn't hesitate to kick a man, even a police officer, when he went down. By two that morning, with a pub off Hedon Road already fired by someone or other and several bleeding women telling desk sergeants how they had been raped in some dark air-raid shelter by one of 'them Yankees', Hull had come to realize that all was not sweetness and light with this new 'special relationship' that Winnie had brought about.

Not that the originator of the 'special relationship' was worried by the events in Hull, even if he had learned of them. He was waiting for other news from the north-east port: the details of what the Irish spy, now in police custody, might have revealed to the Hun.

The man from Special Branch was quiet but dangerous – Inspector Thwaite of the Hull constabulary could see that, as the London tec looked through the details of the arrested man with him.

'We soon cottoned on to him, once we'd found the dead Yank in the air-raid shelter. I mean it's not every navvy who reads the *Irish Times*. He indicated the crumpled piece of bloodstained newspaper found at the scene of the crime. 'We got his prints and they matched with the prints we found at the building site. The foreman there soon pinpointed Kerrigan, if that's his real name, for us. He'd only taken the boat from Holyhead a week or so ago.'

Sombrely the Special Branch man nodded his head. 'I see,' he said. 'And the message he was trying to send when you attempted to apprehend him?'

Inspector Thwaite's jaw hardened when he

thought of the poor dead cop, who had been shot and killed in cold blood. 'Not decoded as yet, sir. The local naval HQ is working on it. But they say his radio was tuned to some German secret service station in Germany.'

'Hamburg?'

'Yes, that's it, Hamburg.'

The Special Branch man rubbed his heavy unshaven jaw; he had not had time to shave. The RAF had flown him straight from London to the nearest airforce field, at Bridlington.

Outside in the packed cells a drunken American voice was crying, 'I want to see my lawyer,' to which a dour East Yorkshire voice replied, 'Put a sock in it, will yer.'

The Special Branch man didn't seem to notice. Finally he broke his silence. 'Well, we'd better have a look at him. We know enough already, I think, though he might tell us a bit more of what he knew of the Yanks arriving here. But I doubt it, these Irish blokes are hard buggers.'

Inspector Thwaite felt for his knuckle-duster, which he always kept in his pocket for such occasions. 'Let me loose on the bugger, sir, and I'll soon have him singing like a bloody yellow canary.'

The man from London shook his head.

'That wouldn't be democratic.'

'Fuck democratic! He shot one of my people in cold blood.'

The Special Branch man didn't seem to hear. Londoners, Thwaite told himself scornfully, they allus go by the book.

Five minutes later they paused at the end of the long corridor, which smelled of stale urine and human misery, in front of the hospital cell, guarded by a policeman armed with a revolver, an unusual sight in Hull police station.

'Anything, Jones?' the local inspector asked.

'Not a sausage, sir,' the guard replied. 'I wish he'd have started larking about like them bloody Yanks down there. I'd have soon settled the murderous bugger's hash for him.'

The Special Branch man frowned. He told himself that it was fortunate that he had been called to this godforsaken place. If he hadn't been, the Irishman on the other side of the door might have suffered an 'unfortunate accident while in police custody', as they usually phrased it. But then one didn't need a crystal ball to realize that the locals would hate the man who had murdered a colleague with a passion. He might not even have survived the night.

'All right, Jones,' Thwaite commanded, 'let's have a look at the bugger.'

The other policeman fumbled with his keys, saying, 'I didn't give him anything, as you ordered, Inspector, not even a drink of water. Mind you, sir, he didn't even call for nowt...'

'Good work, Jones,' the inspector commented as the door of the hospital cell squeaked open rustily to release the pungent smell of ether and Dettol disinfectant.

The two of them blinked and accustomed their eyes to the gloom of the room, focusing on the motionless figure lying on the chipped white steel hospital cot.

Almost at once the Special Branch man knew there was something wrong. Why was the prisoner lying on the blanket and not under it? Why were the tubes of the drip at the right side of his bed hanging loose? Even as Thwaite snarled, 'All right, Kerrigan, don't bugger about. Open yer eyes and get ready to answer a few questions or it'll be the worse—'

'I don't think the prisoner will be answering any questions this morning, Inspector, the Special Branch man interrupted quietly. 'Look.' Indicating the dull crimson hospital blanket, he added, 'Full of blood. He's dead.'

'Well I'll be buggered,' Thwaite exclaimed.

The Special Branch man told himself, No, you won't. *I'll* be, once Churchill hears about this.

Four

'Gentlemen,' Churchill pontificated, 'on Saturday 9th August 1941 I met the President of the United States, Franklin Delano Roosevelt, at the Bay of Placentia on the other side of the world. At that time, our world was in virtual ruins. We had been thrown out of France and it looked as if we might well be thrown out of the Mediterranean soon, too. In short, we could have been defeated at any time.'

The listening admirals looked stern. They knew only too well what the PM meant. Then it had been only their own Royal Navy that had staved off defeat at great cost.

'There at the Bay of Placentia we had a historic meeting. It decided the fate of democracy. It symbolized the deep underlying unities which stir and, at decisive times, rule the English-speaking peoples throughout the world. Indeed, I would be presumptuous enough to say that that meeting symbolized something more majestic – namely the marshalling of the good forces of the world against the evil forces, which then and now seem so formidable and triumphant and which have cast their cruel spell over the whole of Europe.' He paused and let his words sink in.

Naturally the admirals were patriots and firm believers in Churchill and his dogged determination to win the war. But they were men of the world, too, and cynical about politicians, as their type usually were. So they accepted the rhetoric and the fine sentiments, yet at the same time they wondered why they had been summoned here so hastily from Whitehall and why Churchill was indulging in so much window-dressing.

A moment later the Prime Minister told them.

'As you all know, the first American supply convoy has now arrived at Hull. In a matter of hours it will sail for Murmansk as agreed, escorted solely by ships of the Royal Navy. No American warships will be involved.' He paused momentarily before launching into the real reason for having summoned them here this afternoon. 'We now have reliable intelligence that the Germans have comprehensive intelligence on the convoy and are already taking preparatory measures to launch a full-scale attack on it once it sails within reach of their northern bases. As far as we can ascertain, they will attack by U-boat and aircraft, perhaps by surface craft, if they are prepared to risk their remaining capital ships, by their cruisers and battle cruisers, too.'

He paused briefly and looked at his admirals, all hard, battle-experienced men, some of whom he had known since World War One and all of whom had served under him at the beginning of the present war when the Royal Navy had welcomed him back as First Lord with a heartfelt 'Winnie's back!' Unlike the Army's generals, these were men of independent minds. They wouldn't accept orders tamely if they thought them wrong. Still, Churchill had to try, though he knew his listeners had little time for the machinations of politicos and the kind of political manoeuvre he was trying to carry out now.

'So what are we going to do about these Americans, gentlemen? Do we let the

Germans have their way with their ships completely? Losses they will incur, do what we may, and although the unfortunate American merchant sailors will suffer, those losses will indicate to my friend President Roosevelt just how costly this war in Europe is. Still, the blame will be on us, as far as the American public will see it, if their losses are too great.' He looked around at their hard faces and posed that overwhelming question – the reason for which he had had them summoned here: 'Can we allow that convoy to be protected by a mere handful of mine-sweepers, destroyers, corvettes and the like, and the handful of antiquated planes that the Fleet Air Arm can throw in to their defence, or do we involve our own capital ships, as risky as that could be against German dive-bombers?' He paused, breathing a little harder with the effort of formulating that long question.

It was met by a heavy, brooding silence, broken only by a section of the Guards' fife-and-drum corps marching smartly to the tune of 'The British Grenadiers' on the Horse Guards outside.

Pound, a heavyset, somewhat ponderous admiral, spoke first. 'Sir, I can understand your problems. Please understand ours. We have undertaken to assist the Eighth Army in the Med. In the Atlantic we're doing the Americans' job for them because their Admiral King hates our guts and won't organize the US navy into running a proper convoy system. So we're bearing the brunt of that job and finally we are on call, especially the Home Fleet up in Scapa Flow, just in case the German capital ships, the *Gneisnau* and the like, attempt to break out of their French Channel bases. The Royal Navy's capital ships are, to put it mildly, stretched to the limit.' He stopped abruptly, his heavy, lined face revealing nothing of his innermost thoughts, while all around him there came a murmur of agreement from his fellow admirals.

Churchill frowned. He had expected his admirals to disagree. The navy was always jealous of its precious ships. But he had not expected such a total refusal. Naturally he knew he could have ordered them to produce the ships to protect the American convoy. But it might have affected the British public if it came out that the already hard-pressed British fleet, already losing ship after ship in the Med, had suffered grievous losses in ships and men protecting an American convoy carrying supplies to

Russia. What would the average man in the street think of that, when the British rations were down to a bare minimum, with plans already being prepared to ration potatoes, if things didn't improve before the winter was out?

Churchill gave in. He shrugged slightly and lit a cigar. The admirals relaxed a little. They could see that Winnie was going to allow them to husband their resources; the battleships and cruisers would remain in the protection of Scapa Flow for the time being. Thus it was that Pound, as hard and bluff as he was, asked, 'And the current protection for this Yankee convoy, sir?'

Churchill took the cigar out of his mouth. 'Not much, I'm afraid. The scrapings of the barrel really. I believe the defence force consists of a minesweeper and couple of those antiquated American four stackers.'

At the back of the room, a junior rear-admiral sniggered. 'Ah, one of those *gifts*,' he emphasized the word pointedly, 'for which the Yanks charged us half our Caribbean bases.'*

*In 1940 in return for the use of these bases the USA gave Britain fifty WWI destroyers that had been 'mothballed' for years.

Churchill didn't appear to notice. He continued with 'and perhaps four corvettes'.

Pound grunted and summed up the feelings of his fellow admirals, 'Poor buggers, PM, they'll be wiped out – *totally*.'

The meeting was over and Churchill had lost. The convoy would have to take care of itself. In essence, the American convoy and its Royal Navy escort were doomed.

Slumped in his car as he drove out of London to inspect the ruins left by the Luftwaffe raid on the cathedral city of Bath, a job he didn't like but which he knew he had to undertake to keep up the people's morale, he pondered the whole business of Anglo-American relations. He was half-American himself through his mother and thought he understood the American psyche. He felt they were, on the whole, a fine people, generous to an extreme in some cases. But the stock had been watered down by successive generations of immigrants, and the old English values which the Pilgrim Fathers and the other early English settlers of that great country had brought with them had been watered down too.

Roosevelt was of that stock, though his ancestry was Dutch. Yet all the same Churchill felt that he was a politician, admittedly a great one, who couldn't be trusted. FDR had his own agenda, which didn't include ensuring that the British empire survived the war; something that he, Churchill, was determined should happen. After all, his doctrine of the 'special relationship' had been based on America helping Britain to avoid defeat and reclaim her overseas possessions that had been lost to the enemy, in particular the Japs.

Now he was faced with the first real test in action of the coalition and for the life of him he hadn't an idea how the American public would react if it ended in disaster. He could hazard a guess at how FDR would react. He'd distance himself from any debacle because the American elections and his own political future were more important than success in battle some three thousand miles away in Europe in places that most Americans had never even heard of. After all, in nine months of war the American home front had suffered exactly five civilian casualties, whilst in Britain well over fifty thousand men, women and children had been killed by German bombing.*

He sighed, brow creased with worry, feeling himself being overcome by that familiar 'black dog', as he called it, which attacked him in moments of despair and pessimism. What was he to do about that damned convoy? But his mind refused to function and think the problem through.

So the great man slumped, wrapped up in a cocoon of his gloomy thoughts, heading for the scene of another disaster to his hard-pressed people, Hull and the convoy forgotten for a moment, wondering if Britain would ever again see the light at the end of the dark tunnel of total war...

By the afternoon of that same day, while a seemingly supremely confident Churchill marched between the smoking ruins of the old cathedral city, strange old-fashioned square bowler raised on the end of his stick as he waved to the cheering crowds of bombed-out citizens, the news of the admirals' refusal to use their capital ships in the defence of the 'Yank convoy' had filtered down naval channels and reached the flag officer in charge of Hull. Within the hour he had summoned Lt Commander Donaldson to his HQ, which to the dour Scot seemed to

*The Americans had been killed by a Japanese fire balloon, launched by a Japanese submarine way out in the Pacific and which had drifted to land on the US West Coast.

124

resemble a madhouse. Staff officers, red faced and sweating, hurried back and forth, telephones jingled, teleprinters clattered, and the ops room with the big charts of the North Atlantic on the walls was full of American merchant skippers, all seemingly speaking at the tops of their voices.

Hurriedly a worried-looking flag officer guided Donaldson into his office and shut the door firmly in an attempt to drown out the racket. He mopped the sweat from his damp red face and indicated that the skipper of the *Black Swan* should sit down, saying, 'Light up if you wish, Donaldson. I'd like to offer you a pink gin, but some of my junior officers are such prigs. They wouldn't like it.'

Donaldson touched his left pocket and momentarily savoured the comforting feel of his silver whisky flask. 'Didna fash yersen, sir. I'm taken care of. Where's the fire?' He indicated the crazy outside room.

'All hell's been let loose since we learned that their Lordships are not going to help us out with their bloody capital ships.' His temper and frustration burst through momentarily. 'You'd think the buggers owned them personally.' Hurriedly he explained to Donaldson how the admirals had reacted to Churchill's proposal and that somehow the

American merchant skippers had got hold of the news. Most of them had accepted the information without too much protest. But a couple of them, under the leadership of Captain Schurz, the tanker skipper, who still spoke English tainted by the accent of his native Germany, had come to the Flag Office to protest, at one time even refusing to sail. The flag officer had calmed them, but, as he now added, 'Donaldson, we've got to do our best for the poor buggers, especially that tanker skipper. He'll be the Hun's prime target of course.'

'Of course. What can I do?'

'Now I don't have to tell you your job, Donaldson. If it hadn't been for that unfortunate business in North Africa early this year you might well have been doing my job instead of commanding a somewhat broken-down old minesweeper.' He looked away as he referred to the nasty business with the French in Algeria, but Donaldson, hard man that he was, continued to look him squarely in the face. That episode was history now. It was the future that mattered.

'All the same, you've never done the Murmansk Run before, Donaldson, so let me fill you in.' He rose and crossed to the smaller chart behind his desk. 'The convoy will sail the usual route,' he began, tracing it with a well-manicured finger. 'Iceland, Bear Island, the Barents Sea, etcetera. But the real trouble will start once you're past Bear Island – it always does. If the Russkis wanted to help it would be there that they would start. But I'll bet you a fiver that you won't see a single Red Fleet ship or plane till you're practically in Kola Bay. We're risking our lives to bring them supplies—' Suddenly he looked sombre. 'We've already lost ten thousand sailors between Hull and Bear Island.' He shrugged and then added, 'Now we're faced with another dubious ally – the Yanks. But, just as with the Russkis, we've got to do our best with them. So this is *your* first problem.' He looked directly at Don-aldson, almost challengingly, as if he were seeing the pale-faced Scot for the first time.

'It is, sir?'

'The mouth of the Humber. The Hun is not so wooden-headed as some of our folk think he is. He's up to all sorts of monkey tricks. Now we're expecting real trouble after Bear Island. But what if he tries something new before the convoy is barely under-way?'

For a man who was worn out with alcohol, his imprisonment in North Africa and the general burden of three years at war, Donaldson reacted remarkably quickly. 'You mean mine the entrance to the Humber, sir.'

'Very smart, Donaldson. Hit the nail on the head first time. That's what Intelligence thinks the Hun might well do. Their recce planes have been over Spurn Point right up to Withernsea for the last few days. So this is what we want you to do... .'

Five

The *Black Swan* was about to leave the lock now and enter the Humber proper. Standing on the deck of the ship supervising the lock detail, CPO Tidmus kept an eye on his missus, who shouldn't have been there in the first place – how she'd got by the naval police at the gate to the dock was beyond him. Now, with her head muffled in a shawl, she was standing out of the bitter wind in the shelter of the lock-keeper's office, touching her eyes with her handkerchief. Ever since he had been posted back to his native town she had seen him off like this every time the *Mucky Duck* had sailed, as if this might be the last time she'd see him.

'Silly old devil,' he whispered to himself affectionately, as the dockies on the quay began to cast off the hawsers and the lock creaked open. To the rear of the old ship, a matelot was crooning, *'When that man is dead and gone ... some day the news will flash ... Satan with a small moustache is asleep beneath the lawn ...When that man is dead and gone...'*

Tidmus swung round. 'Stop that ruddy racket,' he called. 'Can't hear mesen ruddy well think.'

'Sorry, Chiefie. Just trying to keep myself happy,' the HO man said.

'Well, bloody well keep yersen happy in yer own bloody time,' Tidmus called back, and then he turned round again to discover his wife had vanished and the *Mucky Duck* was passing through the lock, bumping against the rubber tyres meant to protect her hull. Tidmus knew it was a sloppy performance, but what could you expect from a gash crew like this? Then he forgot the crew, his wife, Hull and everything associated with the land.

They were going to sea again, and once more he was seized by the old feeling, a mixture of apprehension and adventure. He'd always felt like that ever since he had been a young matelot, wearing the straw hat of the old navy and carrying out his duties in bare feet in all weathers. The sea and war could be treacherous but the combination of the two always brought something exciting in a lethal sort of way.

It was the same feeling that animated Smythe as he stood on the bridge, next to Donaldson, watching how he handled the old tub with its difficult steering. The ship's number one had been evacuated the day before with the common seaman's complaint: a bleeding ulcer. Now he and the skipper were the only officers. One day soon, he'd have to share the steering on the *Mucky Duck* with CPO Tidmus when the skipper was off-watch and he needed to know a lot more than he did before that time arrived. So far, it seemed to him, everything that he had learned at Dartmouth counted for precious little in a ship on active service like this old tub.

At that moment it seemed to the callow young officer that his life had changed abruptly. Mummy, prep school and Dartmouth and all the values associated with them were the past. The great adventure of real life had commenced. He was about to test his existence against the lethal violence of the enemy. A few minutes ago he had been a boy. Now he was to become a man.

Other craft, mostly the small warships that would escort the convoy, started to sound their sirens in praise, and even the dockies cheered the departing ship, which they knew was leaving Hull to do battle with the enemy. Young Smythe straightened his shoulders proudly. He was someone at last. He was going to war like his dead father and his father before him.

Out of the corner of his eye, busy as he was with the deck watch, CPO Tidmus caught a glimpse of the young sub-lieutenant as he squared his shoulders and thrust out his chin defiantly as if he were old Admiral Jellicoe himself, and grinned. Once he had been like that, full of piss and vinegar, proud of himself and the service to which he belonged. But today if he had tried to square his shoulders like young Smythe every bone in his body would have squeaked in protest. Still, what a good lad the young officer was. As long as England produced officers like him, the country had nothing to fear.

Donaldson's thoughts as he brought the old tub into the central channel were not so sanguine. The Yankee ships which lined the route they would take to the exit of the Humber were silent. They didn't seem to notice the lone craft that would lead their way. Unlike the Royal Navy craft, their crews didn't cheer the men sailing out to do battle. Indeed, there seemed a sullen silence about the American ships. Here and there a crewman leaned over the railway, smoking moodily and looking at the water without interest, taking no notice of the *Black Swan*. He sensed the Yanks didn't have much heart for this trip to Murmansk, although their skippers wouldn't have the slightest idea of what happened to the convoys on the Murmansk Run. Not that he knew much about such convoys, having never taken part in one of them. But he *did* know about the casualties. If the convoy was lucky and was protected by fog or snow and hail as they approached Russian waters, the skippers of the merchant ships might be lucky and get away with thirty per cent casualties. If the convoy was unlucky and sailed in that bright hard sunshine and perfect blue sky that one sometimes encountered in northern waters, even in winter, casualties might mount to sixty to seventy per cent. Indeed, in a recent run the Royal Navy commodore in charge had turned tail and abandoned his convoy altogether. His flight had been hushed up to the general public, but he had been court-martialled and dismissed from the service. A month later he had committed suicide.

Donaldson's red, bloated old drinker's face hardened. Such a thing would not happen to him. He had made a bad mistake once – that was the reason he had been reduced to commanding this old tub. He wouldn't make another.

An hour later, just after the scruffy cook had served hot cocoa to those on the crowded bridge, the early winter dusk began to close in. It hid the ugly mud banks of the Humber and the thin line of shingle that curved inwards to Spurn Point.

Now as the dimmed-out shore lights and those on the channel's buoys began to blink on and, in the increasing swells, the bells on the buoys started to toll, the harsh northern vista seemed almost beautiful to young Smythe.

It was different from the softer aura of southern England, where he had lived and trained. There was something harder and more masculine about the sight. But whatever it was, he knew, this would be his last glimpse of England for a month – perhaps even for ever, but that was a possibility he was not prepared to dwell on.

His reverie was interrupted by Sparks, the radio signalman. He stood there, slightly uneasy at being on the bridge with the officers, holding a pad and pencil. 'Sir?' he said.

Smythe turned, surprised. 'Yes?' he queried. 'What is it, signalman?'

'Thought you'd like to send the signal, sir. The lads thought you might bring us luck, being the youngest officer on board.' The signalman blushed like Smythe always did, but why Smythe couldn't imagine.

'Signal?' Then he remembered the drill from his days at Dartmouth. That was one thing they were keen on at the naval college: the maintenance of naval traditions dating back to the time of Nelson himself. 'Of course. Give me the pad.'

'And the pencil, too, sir,' Sparks reminded him, 'or perhaps I should do it, sir. If I get it wrong, you won't have to take the can back.'

For a moment Smythe was tempted to be angry, then he realized the crew, just like the old chiefie, were attempting to support him. 'All right, you do it, Sparks. Are you ready?'

Sparks nodded.

Smythe wet his lips and began to dictate his first message from his first ship in his first combat patrol. 'To Flag Officer in Charge, Hull,' he said, 'from HMS *Mucky*...' He corrected himself quickly and Sparks smiled winningly. '*Black Swan*... Sailed in accordance with your 2010 ... stroke ... eighty-four ... stroke zero zero...' Then, as Sparks scribbled away, a dewdrop at the end of his long nose threatening to drop on the pad at any moment, Smythe felt an urgent need to come out of his timid shell and be a man of independent thought and action. He raised his voice and added, 'Please wish the old *Mucky Duck* lots of luck.'

Sparks looked up startled. 'Cripes, sir, that flag officer is a bit of a tartar. I don't think he'd like that, er, "Mucky Duck" bit, if I may be so bold as to say.'

'You may, Sparks. But keep it in.'

'Yessir.'

'While the radioman scribbled down the end of the message, Smythe, feeling very proud of himself, added, 'After all, if we don't come back it won't matter what the flag officer in charge thinks of me, and if we do we'll all probably be collecting chestfuls of gongs, going down to Buck House for tea and biscuits and chats with the King.'

Sparks grinned and said, 'If you say so, sir.' With that and a kind of hasty salute he was off. Within the hour, the details of Smythe's signal to the flag officer, Hull, would be all around the little ship.

Nearby, at the wheel, Commander Donaldson heard the exchange and wondered a little at the new boy. He'd get a good rollicking from naval HQ once they got back to Hull, that is if they got back. Then he dismissed Smythe and concentrated on the darkening horizon and the Walrus that that same flag officer, Hull, had promised him.

Book Three

The First Blood

One

'J'attendrais le jour et la nuit,' the sad woman's voice intoned out of the big French radio set on the zinc-covered bar, as they sat there in their wicker chairs enjoying the last of the autumn sunshine. *'J'attendrais toujours son retour.'*

Kapitanleutnant Horst Hartung, already clad in the leather overalls he would wear when they sailed from Brest, told himself as he sipped his pastis that he would always associate wartime France with that sad little sentimental song in years to come, if there were any years to come for him.

Next to him Klausen, his engineer, put down his glass of fizzy beer and lamented, 'Nice tits, nice arse, nice pins ... Pity I'm broke, Hartung.' He indicated the whores sauntering back and forth in front of the waterfront cafés soliciting trade from the eager young submariners soon to sail once the tide in the estuary was right. 'I mean, look at that young arse-with-ears. He's going at it like a shitty fiddler's elbow,' he added enviously, pointing to the young sailor, his pants halfway down his skinny white rump, pumping himself back and forth into a girl, her skirt held up around her chest in the doorway opposite. 'Shouldn't be allowed – it's indecent. Too good for a lower-deck rating.' He took another sip of his beer, face suddenly sour.

Hartung laughed. 'You're only jealous, Klausen.'

'Not really, skipper. As soon as we get back and I get my pay and allowances I'm going to fall in love with the nearest pavement pounder, I can tell you that on my word of honour. I'll hand her my pay and I'll say, "Beloved, just take a look at the deck cos you'll be looking at the ceiling for the rest of our honeymoon." ' He sighed at the thought and Hartung, his lean young face relaxed for a moment, laughed at the dreamy look on the younger man's face. 'Harvest the good life before death harvests us, eh?'

Klausen nodded in the way all submariners did when they used the old U-boat man's saying. He knew, like Hartung, that the average underwater sailor had a fifty per cent chance of surviving more than a couple of wartime patrols; the U-boat death rate was appalling. Still, there were always eager young lads to volunteer for what they thought at the start was the glamorous life of the underwater sailor. Indeed, Admiral Doenitz had made that point that very morning as he had addressed the six crews of the wolfpack inside the great echoing concrete submarine pen at Brest. 'Sailors,' he barked in his sharp Prussian voice once they had been stood at ease, 'comrades! This night you will sail as part of the biggest attack on a Tommy convoy yet launched. Pull this off and I will personally give each and every one of you three days' leave in Paris, all expenses paid.'

'Those poor buggers of us who survive,' one of the old petty officers, heavy with medals, whispered under his breath.

Hartung had heard the comment and thought it came from one of his own crew, but he said nothing. A few cynics among all these new greenbeaks that now made up his team wasn't a bad thing. Their attitude to the U-boat war helped to keep the new boys on the straight and narrow.

'I shall not belabour the point,' Doenitz had continued, his breath fogging about his wolfish face in the cold air of the great submarine pen, 'but I'll say this. One wolfpack in the right place to kill the enemy in large numbers is as good as a whole *Wehrmacht* division of stubble-hoppers, of some fifteen thousand men. Mr Churchill, that drunken sot, will –' he grinned, baring his sharp yellow teeth like a savage animal – 'I am sure testify to that.' Doenitz had paused and then continued with, 'This is the largest operation launched by the U-boat weapon and the Luftwaffe against the Tommies' convoys so far. I don't know about the flyboys, those pilots are a law unto themselves, but I am sure my boys will show them how the Tommies ought to be killed.' He had clicked to attention, his face adopting its usual severe expression again, and raised his hand to his gold-braided cap in salute. 'U-boat men – comrades – I salute you!'

At his side the naval band had struck up *'Deutschland Über Alles'*, and without orders the crews had come to attention too, and as one had commenced singing in their deep young voices, *'Deutschland ... Deutschland...'* even Hartung, the old hare, who had been through this departure ceremony more times than any of the wolfpack commanders, was moved – so much so that the tears

142

had sprung to his red-rimmed eyes.

That had been in the morning. Since then he and his men had celebrated what the U-boat men called the 'last fuck before heaven – or hell', drunk as much as they dare if they were not on first watch when their boat sailed, and had enjoyed the simple pleasure of breathing in clean sea air: a pleasure unknown to them before they had learned what it was to spend days enclosed in a steel tube that stank of stale cooking, wet clothing, human sweat, and, sometimes, abject fear.

But now the time had come to leave. Reluctantly Horst Hartung downed the last of his pastis, flung the last of his greasy French franc notes on the counter, nodded to the sharp-eyed madame behind the bar and with Klausen sauntered out followed by the notes of the syrupy song *'J'attendrais'*.

But even as the two of them followed the rest of the crews heading for the pen and the final briefing before they sailed, the dirge-like wail of the air-raid sirens over Brest coming in from the sea to the west and heading straight for the submarine bunkers told the veteran skipper and his engineer officer that something was wrong. As Klausen expressed hurriedly before they broke into a run, 'The buck-toothed Tommies have rumbled us, Hartung ... The tea-drinking pigdogs are on to us already.' Then the two young officers were running all out for the protection of the great submarine pen as the first of the two-engined Blenheim bombers came tearing in at zero feet, bomb doors open, machine guns spitting lethal white fire...

Five hundred miles away to the north, Donaldson, too, was suddenly alarmed by the steady drone of aircraft engines. A sea fret had set in once they had cleared Spurn Point and a white mist had settled low over the water. But Donaldson guessed that above it the moon was shining; he could see the silver shimmer on top of the fog. Now he craned his head to one side, as he reduced speed, knowing already he was in danger; not from above, but from below. If the Jerries had already dropped mines at the exit to the Humber he had at this moment no way of knowing. That is why he urgently needed the assistance of the plane that the flag officer, Hull, had informed him would help once he reached the open sea.

Automatically he reduced speed and ordered, 'Quiet please,' and then, 'Starboard lookout, keep your eyes peeled. Should be a

Walrus,'

'Aye aye, sir,' the lookout replied, pulling down his Balaclava hood so that he could hear better as the noise of the plane grew ever closer.

Smythe, standing next to Donaldson on the little bridge, couldn't restrain his curiosity any longer. The name 'Walrus' was unfamiliar to him. So he ventured, 'Are we expecting a plane, sir?'

Donaldson restrained his fiery temper just in time. He was going to need the green sub-lieutenant before this trip was over, he knew. It wouldn't do to get the young fellow's back up at this stage of the game. So he explained, 'Yes, a Walrus – that's a damned antiquated push-engine seaplane. Should have been scrapped years ago. But you know our parsimonious rulers in the House of Commons. Anyway, Smythe, this particular Walrus is fitted with a new kind of powerful air-to-ground searchlight. It should penetrate even this damned sea fret.'

Before Smythe could ask why and make even more of a fool of himself, CPO Tidmus stepped in and said, 'Then we can see the mines, if there are any of the bloody deadly things.'

'Yes,' the captain agreed. 'Then we'll be

able to sweep more quickly and get the convoy sailing into the North Sea faster than the Jerries at the other side of what my old grandfather used to call the "German Ocean" anticipated. It might give us just a slight edge on them and upset their assault timetable. Anything to give us a few miles of peace without—' He stopped short as on the deck below the soaked, freezing lookout called, 'Aeroplane engine to the starboard. Zero red...'

But Donaldson was no longer listening. Hurriedly he switched on the main light on the blacked-out bridge. 'It's the Walrus,' he exclaimed.

Next moment he was proved correct. For an instant the whole ship was drenched in a glaring incandescent white light, which blinded those on the bridge so that Tidmus had only a moment to identify the plane almost above them, crying, 'It's the Walrus, sir,' before he was completely blinded by the tremendous light and was forced to close his eyes and shut it out.

'Good show,' Donaldson cried with un-usual enthusiasm for him, and both his own bridge light and the one from above went out, leaving them all blinking for a second in the sudden darkness.

'Stop engines,' Donaldson commanded, speaking down the tube to the engine room and clicking the bridge telegraph back and forth. The *Black Swan* proceeded a little further as the throbbing of her engines died away before she came to a stop to wallow in the swell. In front of them the Walrus, glimpsed as a black shadow as it came gliding through the white fog, came into land and Smythe watched the meeting entranced, telling himself this was a great adventure, something he could tell his kids about, if he ever managed to find a woman and have what his mummy called delicately 'sexual congress' with her to produce those kids.

Suddenly, startlingly, the slow chug-chug of the ancient seaplane's single engine was drowned by the vicious roar of two high-powered ones.

'What the hell!' Donaldson exclaimed, pale face suddenly red with fury. His outburst was cut off by the rat-tat-tat of machine-gun fire. Red and white tracer zipped through the darkness in a lethal morse. Smythe gasped. Pieces were flying from the old seaplane in a metal rain. He caught a glimpse of the cockpit shattering into a gleaming spider's web with the pilot's face behind frantic with fear. Smoke started to pour from that single engine below the biplane's wings. Next moment the Walrus's nose went down and, to Tidmus's horror, the old plane went straight down right into the sea. Next moment a dark shape hurtled by, the plane's guns still blazing fire, and zoomed up into the moonlit sky in wild triumph.

CPO Tidmus reacted speedily. 'Look alive down there on deck!' he yelled, cupping his hands around his mouth. 'Man the Bren gun... . You, lookout, grab a boathook and see if you can fish the poor sod of a pilot out of the drink. At the double now...'

Donaldson reacted equally speedily. He swung round on a bemused Smythe, who was suddenly realizing he had just had his first taste of action and that he had actually seen a British plane shot down by the enemy. 'Get Sparks up here smartish. Send this signal to Flag Officer, Hull.' Hastily the young sub-lieutenant took out his notebook. 'Sir?'

'Walrus shot down at rendezvous,' Donaldson dictated at the top of his voice as he steered the craft again, searching as he did so for the missing Walrus pilot. 'Obvious our code broken. Suggest alert convoy immediately.' He paused. 'Encode and get it off toot sweet. Headquarters must know at once that we've been compromised.'

Five minutes later the alert situation was all over. There was no sign of the Walrus pilot – he couldn't have lasted long in the freezing waters of the North Sea anyway, and the German plane that had attacked it had long vanished, back to its field in Belgium. Suddenly Smythe felt a strange sensation of being let down.

Two

'Bugger ... bugger me!' CPO Tidmus swore, nearly upsetting his cup of cocoa.

It was dawn. The sky to the east was beginning now to flush a dirty white over the dull grey wash of a sullen North Sea. To left and right on the horizon the escort craft were beginning to form up in the convoy's protective screen. But so far there was no sign of the merchantmen coming down the mine-free lane that the *Black Swan* had checked through the long night even without the help of the shot-down Walrus.

'The buggers are on to us right off,' Tidmus continued as he and Smythe stood on the foredeck watching the escort vessels.

'What buggers?' the young officer queried.

CPO Tidmus contained his rage. He said, 'The Jerries, sir. They've got a bloody shad up already, sod 'em.'

Smythe looked puzzled. '*Shad*, Chiefie?' he queried.

'Yessir. To port, sir. Looks like a four-engined Condor to my tired old eyes.'

Smythe looked in the direction indicated, as the alarm bell rang and a petty officer behind them yelled, 'Shad, lads. Keep yer eyes peeled.'

'Why shad, Chiefie?' Smythe asked, as always puzzled. Dartmouth had not really prepared him for active service and it had certainly not readied him for the lingo talked by the matelots; it was almost, at times, as if they were speaking a foreign tongue.'

'*Shadow*, sir,' Tidmus explained. 'A Jerry plane that observes the convoy as long as they have fuel. They're mostly Condors or Blohm and Voss 138s. We hate 'em like poison. They're allus looking at yer and reporting back to their bases. It's like yer were slipping a link to the old lady and some nosy bugger was peeping through the ruddy window.'

As always Smythe blushed, especially as he hadn't thought that someone who was as old as the grey-haired CPO was would be still having sex.

Tidmus drained the rest of his cocoa while the deck watch slung their steel helmets over their shoulders and the couple of gun crews closed up to their weapons, as if the appearance of the German plane indicated that a battle was soon to commence.

The old CPO relaxed again and gave the young officer a tired smile. 'I remember, sir, a couple of months ago, when we had the old skipper – he was a bit of a card. Anyhow, we was on the Murmansk Run when we copped a Shad. Round and round the bugger went, hour after hour, till the skipper had had enough. So he called up Bunts –' Tidmus meant the ship's signaller – 'and told him to signal the Jerry pilot.' He laughed at the memory. 'And do you know, sir, what he told Bunts to signal?'

Smythe shook his head. 'Go on, tell me, Chiefie.'

Tidmus laughed again. 'He was to signal, "For God's sake, man, can't you fly round the other way. We're getting dizzy the way you're going round and round." Well, would you believe the Jerry altered course and *did* go the other way round. And they say the squareheads have no sense of humour.' For some reason he looked up at the bridge, where a grim-faced Donaldson was still at the wheel, and Smythe guessed that CPO Tidmus was thinking that their present skipper had no sense of humour. He'd never think of signalling an enemy pilot like that.

Indeed, Commander Donaldson would certainly not have even considered such an action. For him there was only one way to deal with the 'squareheads', even if they did have a sense of humour – blast them out of the skies. But at that moment he was not concerned with the sudden appearance of the first shad. His mind was on the non-appearance of the American merchantmen. The lane was clear of mines, the escorts were in position, the weather was all right, but where were the bloody Yanks? He frowned and wished he could go below for a rest and a couple of drams. But at the moment that was out of the question. With his inexperienced crew of HO men and one officer, still wet behind the ears, he needed to be in charge in case there was trouble brewing. Again he cursed to himself, his hands sore from holding the wheel all night, zigzagging back and forth along the shipping lane, risking his ship as he sought the mines. He'd done his best to give the Yanks a good start and enter the North Sea without trouble and now the bigmouthed buggers had still not made an appearance. What was going on back there in the Humber ... ?

The American skippers had sent a delegation to the commodore in charge of the convoy. Orr-Jenkins, big, bluff, red faced and a little pompous, would have called it bloody mutiny if the circumstances had been different and these men had been British merchant seamen. But he had kept his hair-trigger temper under control and offered them a glass of whisky each (which the Yanks had refused in a very churlish manner, he couldn't help thinking, especially as whisky didn't grow on trees these days). Then he had said, 'Well, gentlemen, what brings you to me at this stage of the business? Time is of the essence, you know.'

Schurz, the skipper with the German name and trace of the accent he had brought with him from the Old Country as an immigrant child, acted as spokesman. Straight off, he growled, 'I'll give it to you straight,

153

Commodore, we can't sail under these conditions.'

'What conditions?' the Commodore had asked, fighting to keep his temper under control.

'Those pathetic old ships you've gotten for us as escorts—'

'Some of them are from your own navy.'

Schurz didn't appear to hear. He continued with, 'Hell, if I farted hard, I could blow the bastards out of the water. Besides, we've heard firing to the east. The Krauts are out there already, it seems to us. No, sir, Commodore, we can't sail without better protection than you Limeys can offer us.' There was a murmur of agreement from the other skippers.

Commodore Orr-Jenkins felt his blood pressure climbing. He was about to explode at any minute. But he knew that Churchill was behind this particular convoy, and he wanted to help the great man the best he could. So he said, 'What do you suggest I do, Captain?'

'Postpone our sailing date, Commodore.' Schurz had his answer ready, as if he and his fellow skippers had discussed the matter beforehand.

'And then?'

'Contact the US Navy Department through our embassy in London and get some real American warships instead of those leaky old tin cans of yours.' He looked up challengingly at the big naval officer, jaw jutting, working his cheap unlit cigar from one side of his mouth to the other.

'As simple as that, eh, Captain. We hold up the war for you and your colleagues?'

Irony was wasted on the Americans. 'Yeah, why not? We're Americans after all. We have our rights.'

Commodore Orr-Jenkins had had enough. He felt his face flush a brick red. 'Well, let me tell you something, Captain Schurz, and the rest of you, too. If I had my way I'd put you all in irons. But my power is limited.'

Schurz sniggered. 'Yeah, we thought you'd see reason, Commodore.' There was a murmur of approval from the other skippers.

'But I just have no time for the red tape,' Orr-Jenkins roared, eyes bulging out of his head. 'Just too much bullshit and the tide's turning. So what I'm going to do, Schurz, is this.' He raised his voice even more. 'Sentry,' he bellowed.

The young Marine sentry guarding his office door, bayonet fixed, came in immediately. Without ceremony he pushed his way through the suddenly confused Americans and stamped his right foot down hard so that the equipment on Orr-Jenkins' desk rattled. 'Sir?'

'Arrest that man.' The Commodore pointed a finger, which trembled with rage, at an abruptly pale-faced Schurz. 'Take him away to the cells.'

Schurz nearly swallowed his cheap cigar. 'You ... you can't do that,' he stuttered. 'I'm ... an American.'

'Can't I just?' Orr-Jenkins snapped. 'I can do more. Once you're in the cells, I'm going to call the US naval attaché in London and inform him that I've got a mutiny on my hands. That I am arresting you and am preferring charges under paragraph,' speedily Orr-Jenkins picked a number out of his head – he knew the Yank wouldn't know anything about British law, 'fifty-seven of Naval Regulations in Wartime. It could mean a long spell behind bars for you, Schurz, American or not.'

'Jesus H. Christ,' one of the US skippers exclaimed. 'You wouldn't do that, sir, would you?'

Orr-Jenkins noted the 'sir' and snapped back, 'I certainly would, Captain. No doubt about that.'

Schurz tried to bluster it out. 'But who'd sail your ships for you, if you arrested us, eh?'

Orr-Jenkins looked down at him coldly. 'That would be no problem, Captain Schurz. Our labour exchanges are full of brave ships' captains who have lost their craft at sea, *in battle* – and who are now beached against their wishes. They are just crying out for a ship and a new berth, British or American, they don't mind. He couldn't resist it, but he was so angry at the Americans that he had to turn the knife in the wound. 'They have no prejudices against whom they command, Limey or Yank.'

That was it. The American skippers filed out in silence, shoulders bowed as if in defeat. After they had gone, Orr-Jenkins dismissed the sentry and sat down abruptly, suddenly drained of energy. For a moment or two he sat there, staring at the standard portrait of the King-Emperor in naval uniform on the wall opposite. It gave him an uneasy feeling; he didn't know why.

One thing he did know, however. He had forced the Yanks into sailing, but they didn't like it, or the fact that a 'Limey' had forced them into battle, for that was what the Murmansk Run was. Now they would resent him, perhaps even hate him. So how would they react when the battle commenced and he had to give them orders that they wouldn't like one bit? He could guess and it worried him. Somehow, as things stood now, he felt that this convoy, the first American one, was going to end in a bloody mess.

Half an hour later, changed into his winter gear, he went down to the launch that would take him to his command ship. The convoy could start.

Three

'By the Great Whore of Buxtehude where the dogs piss out of their ribs,' Klausen exclaimed with delight, 'have you ever seen so much meat and no potatoes?'

Next to him as they entered the officers' brothel Hartung grinned at his engineer officer's obvious delight as the sight of so many French whores, most of them naked save for black silk stockings and frilly knickers. They stared back at the two newcomers with professional interest, one or two of them licking their lipsticked lips significantly. It was something not lost on Klausen, who was already half drunk. He exclaimed, 'What a great people the French are. They don't huff and puff like we Germans when we are making love, they use their tongues.'

'Don't mention love,' Hartung chided his comrade mildly. 'Here everything is strictly commercial.' He made the German gesture of counting money with his thumb and forefinger.

It was as if the madam could read Hartung's thoughts, for she hurried from her place behind the big cash register, showing a deal of ample flesh above the black stockings as she got up from the bar stool, rubbing her hands. 'Ah, gentlemen,' she said in accented German, 'what a pleasure to see officers from the submarine service here in Calais. You are a, er, rarity.'

Hartung frowned slightly at her mention of the U-boat arm. How did a common-or-garden whore mother know how to distinguish a submarine officer from one of those jokers who sailed in surface craft? But he dismissed the thought as soon as it had come. This night in Calais he intended to use solely for pleasure before the nasty business of kill or be killed commenced in the North Sea.

The signal diverting the wolfpack to Calais had come totally unexpectedly. They had been cruising through the Channel, taking turns to raise the periscope for short periods and gaze at the white smudge that was England, the home of their arch-enemy, Mr Churchill, the crew members commenting, 'Why don't the Tommies stop in their damn island? *Was haben sie bei uns in Europe zu suchen?*' It was a question for which Hartung had no time to think of an answer for just then the radio signal from Doenitz's HQ had come in and he had had to alter his course immediately and sail for the port of Calais, which although well protected with flak and coastal guns was not the ideal berth for the thin-skinned U-boats of the wolfpacks.

Hartung already knew that the basic plan was for the German E-boats stationed on the island of Texel and the Luftwaffe bomber squadron located outside Amsterdam to worry away at the enemy convoy once it was in the area of the northern Dutch coast. Once this combined force had slowed the Tommies and their Yank allies down and the convoy had reached the deeper waters of the North Atlantic, where the wolfpack could operate with more safety from Allied air attack, they would go into action.

He assumed now after decoding the urgent signal from the 'Great Sea Lord', as the U-boatmen called Doenitz, their beloved commander, that something had temporarily gone wrong with the combined E-boat, Luftwaffe attack in North Holland. Why else would naval HQ direct them to the relatively dangerous berth of Calais, a matter of a couple of score kilometres from the Tommies' airfields in southern England? But personally that was a risk that Hartung was prepared to take. The overnight stay in the old French ferry port would give the men a last chance to let their hair down before the murderous battle of the cruel North Atlantic commenced. He was glad of the respite.

Klausen, the inveterate skirt-chaser, hardly waited for the sleek, clever-eyed madam to say her piece when he pointed to the fat whore seated at the bar. She was dreaming away as if she were in another world, and didn't look very intelligent. But Klausen wasn't after her brain; his mind was concentrating on other parts of her anatomy – and there was certainly plenty of her. Her slip fitted as if she were two sacks of potatoes tied together by a tight belt, which disappeared into the soft pillow of her snow white belly, fringed with black pubic hair. Above it, written in black tattoo, was the old legend, *'Keep off the grass.'*

Klausen chortled happily and said, 'Skipper, can I have her? I'd love to trim her lawn for her!'

'Sure you can,' Hartung agreed, 'but let me have your boot size.'

Klausen looked puzzled. 'Boot size?'

'Yes, just in case you get lost in all that meat.'

'There's no better way to go, Skipper,' Klausen said happily and, pulling his belt tighter, advanced on the fat whore, crying, 'Come on, *ma chérie*, come and try this on for size.' Moments later he was bundling her upstairs in a great hurry, hands already caressing her massive trembling buttocks, as if he couldn't get into bed to dance the mattress polka soon enough.

Hartung took his time, sipping his Ricard slowly. With seven years of the *Kriegsmarine* behind him he had enjoyed plenty of women – mostly paid for, but then U-boat skippers didn't have much time for long-term love affairs. Over the years he had had them all: black, white, yellow and all shades in between. By now he had come to know what he wanted from a woman, even if it was only for an hour or so, and how he could recognize the type who could give him the pleasure he wanted.

At the other end of the bar another whore sat just like that moon-faced one now upstairs making the bedsprings squeak merrily with the eager Klausen. But this one was svelte and slim, fully dressed and drinking a lemonade. In the big mirror behind the counter he could see her eyes. They were green and remote, hinting at depths of sexual perversion – and sadness – which intrigued him immediately. 'What's her name?' he asked the whore-mother.

'Solange,' the Frenchwoman answered. 'She's difficult.'

Hartung imagined she could be. Indeed, at that moment he wondered what she was doing in this lower-rank officers' brothel. She seemed the type who might take up with an elderly general: one who would spoil her, shower her with gifts, show her off to his friends and not make too many sexual demands on her. He rose from his stool, leaving his drink unfinished, suddenly eager to find out what motivated the French-woman, her secrets and how he might use them for his own sexual pleasure.

Above him in the fat whore's shabby room, Klausen was motivated by more basic sexual desires. As soon as she had closed the door, the fat whore had clasped her plump arms around him and stuck her tongue into his ear with professional concupiscence, breathing hard with fake passion. 'Sailorboy want jig-jig?' she had asked in broken German.

'You bet your life,' he had answered eagerly, as she had opened her gown. Almost as if they were falling off her ample body, her fat breasts with their red-painted nipples had dropped into his waiting hands. He had gasped and she had given him a gold-toothed smile, saying, 'You want suck Mama's titties?'

Before he had had time to consider, she had taken her left breast from him and had proffered the sweat-tasting left nipple to the open-mouthed Klausen, who could do little else but suck it or be choked by the massive piece of flesh filling his mouth now.

Somehow he had freed himself from her grasp and had gasped, 'You're supposed to have a yellow card of clean health if you're working in one of these places.'

'Fuck yellow card,' she had snorted. Then, without any further ado, she had dropped on top of him and made the old brass bedstead groan mightily, submerging him in that mountain of warm white blubber. 'Boche,' she whispered as he felt frantically for the part of her anatomy that he desired now with burning lust. 'Dumb bastards. They can't even eat soup with a spoon.' Aloud she cried as if in the ultimate throes of ectasy, *'Je t'aime, chéri!'*

Klausen's experience with the fat whore might have been pedestrian but at least he got his satisfaction from it. As he intended to relate afterwards, 'Did I get the heavy water off my manly chest, comrades ... ? It was dipping it in hot perfumed suds.' For Hartung it was different. The mysterious-looking silver-blonde with her green eyes proved difficult, even disappointing. Of course, she performed all the little sexual tricks that he had come to expect from French pavement pounders, and although she routinely panted and gasped, as if she were in the throes of a grand passion, he could sense that her heart wasn't in the business. Indeed, he felt she resented him in some way.

They parted amicably enough. He bought her a last champagne, gave her some money and kissed her hand gallantly, as if she were some high-born *gradiges Fraulein*, but even as he departed he sensed she had something else on her mind, which left him with a kind of foreboding of a nature that he couldn't quite explain.

Now a silent Hartung and a voluble Klausen plodded up the cobbled road that led by the German bunkers defending the port, heading for their ship's berth. 'I could have eaten it with a silver spoon,' Klausen yelled above the roar of the waves crashing in wild fury against the breakwater, as the wind from the North Sea howled and grew in strength by the instant. Hartung, half listening to his old comrade, told himself that they were in for a storm.

'God, was she good,' Klausen lied. 'She nearly sucked my back collar stud out.'

'Yes,' he answered routinely, wondering why Solange had been so remote despite the big tip he had given her. Whores were usually very grateful when it came to money; after all, that was why they were spreading their legs, wasn't it?

'You know, skipper, she had so much suction, I thought—' Klausen stopped abruptly, faltered in mid-stride and looked down, gap-mouthed, at the sudden red stain spreading across the chest of his navy blue tunic, just above his Iron Cross.

Hartung stopped too. It looked as if Klausen was drunk. His eyes were rolling foolishly, mouth gaping stupidly, as he uttered unintelligible sounds. 'What's the trouble?' he snapped, the whores and his pleasure forgotten. 'What's the matter?'

In the surrounding low hills thunder started to roll round with a soft boom. The wind had sprung up too. Lightning forked an electric blue across the sea. It began to rain.

Klausen looked up at him. Now a thin train of black blood was trickling down the side of his chin. The light was going fast from his eyes. 'I ... I...' he stuttered. Startlingly, without any warning, he tore himself from Hartung's grasp and pitched face-forward on the wet cobbles of the *pavé*.

For a moment Hartung was mesmerized with shock. But only for a moment. From the low sand dune to his right there came the sudden high-pitched burr of a machine pistol. Angry blue sparks ran the length of the road heading straight for him. 'Holy shit!' he cried aloud, for some reason which he couldn't explain later. 'They're firing at me!'

They were, whoever they were. But the U-boat skipper didn't wait to find out. He threw himself into the drainage ditch at the other side of the road, dragging out his little service automatic at the same time, his every nerve tingling electrically, tense and very alert now, as a good U-boat skipper should be.

Cautiously he raised his cap above the top of the drainage ditch. Nothing happened. He poked his head slowly, very slowly over the parapet, pistol at the ready. Nothing, save poor old Klausen, the raindrops beating steadily now on his dead face, eyes staring sightlessly into the dark stormy sky...

Half an hour later he had reported the incident to the *Feld gendarmerie*. The tough military policemen, mostly used these days to prevent sabotage at the docks, went into action at once. They surrounded the brothel. But Madame, and her girls had vanished, leaving behind their frillies and the various bizarre tools of their trade used to stimulate flagging libidos.

Swiftly the big, hard-faced captain of the MP rounded up the neighbours, keeping them standing at attention in the pouring rain as he questioned them, twisting his unlit cheap working man's cigar from one side of his cruel mouth to the other. He didn't get far, as scared as the French civilians were of him. A few volunteered information hoping that the Boche might reward them. Others simply answered questions when they were asked.

Men had come in an old coal-burning bus. They had loaded the women and their hurriedly packed carpetbags, seized a couple of bottles of black market scotch from behind the bar and had been off. 'Where to?' the MP captain had demanded. North had been the consensus of opinion. 'Where north?' he had persisted. He'd received a dozen answers – 'Lille ... Cassel ... the Belgian border...'

In the end he had given up and turning to a now worried as well as very angry Hartung said a little wearily, 'Sign of the times, *Herr Kapitanleutnant*. When we were winning they were one hundred per cent on our side. Hell, a whole division of frogs volunteered to fight with the *Wehrmacht*. Now...' He shrugged. 'The Frogs are having a rethink.' He looked Hartung straight in the eye. 'But I'll tell you one thing. I wouldn't stay here in Calais much longer. By this afternoon, over there,' he jerked his big thumb in the direction of the Channel, 'they'll know about you and your U-boats.'

Hartung nodded wordlessly. His usual good humour vanished as he stared out of the window at that sombre, rain-soaked landscape, with the storm slowly vanishing out to sea. Things, he told himself, weren't going to be as easy as he'd thought.

Four

'Jerries ... Jerries ... Jerries!' the deck lookout yelled urgently. *'Port zero...'* But even as the rating shouted the alarm, Donaldson was throwing up his glasses and looking portside.

Coming out of the mixture of rain and sleet, he could see the Junkers 88s sliding into the gleaming circle of calibrated binoculars. Swiftly he counted them, as Orr-Jenkins in his command ship on the fringe of the convoy was already ordering his 4.5 guns to open fire.

There were nine of them, advancing in two waves. They rolled from side to side to avoid the black puffballs of British flak which were starting to explode all around them. They flew at not more than a hundred feet above the water, churning it up in a white fury with their propwash.

'Balls,' he said to no one in particular, 'now we're in for it.'

But already CPO Tidmus was springing into action. For such an old man his reactions were remarkably fast. He'd already got the Lewis gunners and the ratings manning the Brens ready for action. Now it was the turn of those who crewed the *Black Swan*'s only real weapon.

White tracer started to curve through the rain, gathering speed by the instant, heading straight for the massed formation of German bombers. Already their bomb doors were open, ready to unload their evil black eggs on the fat, ponderous merchantmen below. And they were coming ever faster. Soon Donaldson knew they'd risk the flak by rising higher to drop their bombs and then break off and head for their bases in Holland and southern Norway hell for leather. He shoved Smythe at the wheel to one side with a curt, urgent, 'Let me take the con, son,' and then he was prepared to zigzag, one eye to the heaving sea ahead the other on the two waves of Junkers, which seemed to be coming straight at his old tub.

Now the first bombs were dropping around the American merchantmen. Huge pillars of grey-green water rose into the air, swamping the nearest freighter and blotting it out of view for a moment. Hastily Donaldson prayed it hadn't been hit. If it had, the convoy would have to slow down even more. But a moment later the ship was sliding out of the cascade of seawater unharmed.

Now from all sides came the boom of heavy guns and frantic chatter of machine guns as the attacking planes zoomed in and out of the glowing tracer and the zigzag of exploding shells. But the German pilots were not deterred. They came zooming in time and time again, some of the Junkers seeming to flash parallel to the ships, below the levels of their masts.

Their persistence paid off. Now the Junkers had their first kill. Donaldson swore aloud as one of the smaller Yank merchantmen was hit. She wasn't sinking, for which he thanked God, but her steering was definitely out of control, as the ship, with smoke pouring from her engine, zigzagged crazily. But at that moment Donaldson had no time to concern himself with the stricken American ship.

Down below, just beneath the bridge, a young rating manning the Bren gun on a tripod swung round, spraying the *Mucky Duck*'s superstructure with bullets. Donaldson ducked involuntarily as the slugs cut through the air and tore the bridge's woodwork into matchsticks, the rating dropping to the suddenly bloody deck, still firing in his death throes. 'Young snotty,' Donaldson yelled frantically to an awe-stricken Smythe. 'Get on that gun. Keep her firing. At the double, sir!'

'Yessir.' Smythe woke from his reverie. He had never fired a Bren gun in his life, but this was not the time to tell a crimson-faced Donaldson that. He clattered down the littered steps from the bridge. Everywhere there was debris. The hull was marked with the bright white pockmarks of the Junkers' bullets. As gently as he could he pushed the dead rating to one side, took hold of the hot barrel of the Bren and slapped the magazine to check if it was firmly fixed in the breech. It was. Now he didn't hesitate. He raised the gun, swung the tripod round and, praying that it would fire, aimed it at a Junkers coming in so low that he could see the helmeted figures of the two Germans in the cockpit. He pressed the trigger. The Bren slammed back into his shoulder painfully. He didn't notice. He was too fascinated by the white zigzag of tracer heading straight for the two Germans in the cockpit. In a flash the perspex canopy shattered into a gleaming spider's web. Blinded, the two men fought to keep control of the dive-bomber. Smythe's heart leaped. He had actually fired at the enemy – and hit him! Two years after his father had been killed in action he was actually striking back, though, in essence, the young officer didn't think in those terms. At that moment he was more concerned with his own boldness and amazed at the fact that he had proved himself in battle with the enemy, just like his father and grandfather before him.

But as the Junkers lost height, cherry flames beginning to fleck the oily black smoke, no one seemed to notice his triumph. It appeared that all eyes were focused on the American freighter that was running amok some mile away, posing a real danger to the other American merchantmen.

What happened next, Smythe recalled afterwards, seemed more like an episode in some cinema film than a scene from real life. Utterly detached he and the rest of the men, ignoring the German bombers still attacking, though more weakly now, watched as the maverick freighter, sailing in circles, was racked by explosions. Here and there seamen were diving over the side. Others were attempting madly to launch Carley floats and lifeboats. But time was running out for the freighter – fast. Abruptly a huge volcano of fire vomited smoke that rose straight up some 250 feet into the sky, filled with flying wreckage. A human arm slapped down on the deck not a foot from where a bemused Smythe was poised behind his Bren gun, the damaged Junkers forgotten in the light of this new horror. Then, very slowly, the US freighter slid bow-first into the heaving grey-green sea. Minutes later the Junkers were black spots on the horizon. The first attack on the American convoy was over.

Even now most of the bemused seamen of the *Black Swan* hadn't moved. They had been, it seemed, mesmerized by the events that had just taken place. Smythe forced himself with a sheer effort of willpower to look round him at the ratings, who waited in a heavy silence, broken only by the drip-drip of the rain and the steady beat of the engines.

But as always it was CPO Tidmus, the old salt, who brought the crew back to some sort of normalcy. 'Rum-o, lads!' he called cheerfully. 'Special occasion. Mr Smythe just shot down a Jerry plane. We've got something to celebrate.' He pushed through the throng of ratings staring at the drifting wreckage where the US freighter had been, carrying two mugs of rum and water, one of them for Smythe the other for the captain, standing silently in the battered bridgehouse.

There'll be trouble, Donaldson told himself. The Yanks are going to cause a stink. They've forgotten what war's like. It's been twenty-odd years since they were last clobbered. He paused, and raising his binoculars stared across to where the commodore's ship was turning, flags running up its masts, the signallers busy wagging their own flags. Obviously Orr-Jenkins was trying to reassure the Yanks. He wondered how successful the commodore would be; Donaldson thought he was too stuffily British for the Americans.

He shrugged and said to CPO Tidmus, 'Well, at least our young snotty did well.'

'Yessir, he did.' Tidmus was suddenly sombre as the skipper raised the potent mix of hot water and rum to his lips and took an appreciative sip. 'The weather, sir,' he remarked.

'What about it?

'Well, if we're not lucky with it, and Sparks has just told me we can expect good enough weather for flying, then old Jerry'll be back with his bombers. And he'll keep plastering us all the bloody way – if you'll excuse my French, sir – all the way to Bear Island.' He paused. 'But of course the met people could be wrong. You never know in these latitudes. If we're lucky we could run into a nice pea-souper of a thick fog or even a snow storm. It's cold enough for it.' He shivered suddenly and felt glad that his wife had supplied him with an extra set of woollen drawers and vest. 'With luck.'

'And if we don't strike lucky, Chiefie?' Donaldson, who had never sailed the Murmansk Run before, queried.

'Then we'll have to grin and bear it – a day and a half of hell before we reach Bear Island.' The old petty officer, of whom some of the younger ratings joked he had been the last to kiss Admiral Nelson as he lay dying on the deck of the *Victory*, added, 'After Bear Island it'll all be plain sailing, sir. Roses all the way. Just ice floes, Russkies dropping their bombs on us by mistake – they don't seem much cop at ship recognition – and of course the Jerry U-boats. Them buggers are the killers.'

Donaldson pulled up the collar of his greatcoat and let the warmth coming up from the steaming mug of hot water-and-rum circulate round his face. 'Well, all I can say, Chiefie, is Merry Christmas.'

Tidmus laughed. 'And the same to you, sir, when we see it.'

Five

Churchill had only once listened to that damned arch-traitor Lord Haw Haw before; he had no time for the renegade Irishman's cheap propaganda. But on this raw day at Chequers, with the raindrops lashing the mullioned windows of his study savagely, he had his manservant set up his newfangled portable radio, a present from no less a person than President Roosevelt, and prepared to listen. He was desperate for any scrap of information on the American convoy; what news had already come through from his own sources was very bad, very bad indeed.

So far the Hun had sunk just one American ship. That was bad enough, as the Americans would see it. He personally could bear losses of up to, say, twenty-five per cent of the convoy. That would be sufficient to convince the US Chiefs of Staff that any operations in Europe this side of 1944 would be too costly. On the other hand, losses higher than that might scare FDR. For by now Churchill had come to know the crippled President of the United States better. Once the previous year when he had been the President's guest in the White House, the President had propelled himself in his wheelchair to Churchill's room to discover him completely naked, as was often his habit just after taking a bath. FDR had been embarrassed and was about to back out, but he had stopped the President, saying, 'You see, Mr President, my King's First Minister has nothing to hide from the President of the United States.' FDR had given him his toothy smile and that had been that.

Since that time, however, Churchill had learned more of one of the most powerful men on the globe. FDR, he had discovered, promised everything to everybody and promptly forgot his promises minutes later. So what would he do if the losses of the American convoy became too high and the Great American Public got to know of them, which they would (the US press wasn't censored and didn't feel it had to protect the President)?

'Sir?' it was the voice of his manservant.

'Yes?'

'The German gentleman is about to speak from Radio Bremen now, sir.'

Under other circumstances Churchill would have laughed at that 'German gentleman', but this storm-swept day he was in no mood for laughter. He said, 'Please turn the volume up.'

In an instant that familiar snarl, that harsh, incisive, mocking voice swept into the study, drowning out the sound of the rain and the atmospherics, 'Ger-many calling ... Germany calling.'

Churchill waited, sipping his brandy and puffing at his double Havana. As usual Lord Haw-Haw went through the list of cities bombed, naming names, giving the time on the local town hall clocks and details of prominent buildings destroyed – all the stuff that his British listeners were eager to hear;

and details that were censored by the British. Churchill, the orator and great anecdotalist, realized just how effective it all was, this mixture of half-truths, facts and outright lies. It was just the stuff that the gullible listener would swallow hook, line and sinker.

Suddenly Lord Haw-Haw's tone changed. Now the snarl had become authoritarian. 'Ladies and gentlemen, I have to tell you some serious news concerning your cousins from beyond the seas, as Mr Churchill calls them, though I must point out that most of them are probably Jews, just like that crippled Jew Roosenblum in the White House. At this moment some of these Yankees are sailing through German waters to aid the Bolsheviks in Russia. They will never reach the so-called Red paradise. The German armed forces will see to that accursed country soon. In the meantime the full weight of the Luftwaffe and the *Kriegsmarine* will descend upon these cheeky Yankees. You can rest assured that German arms will triumph. Yes, ladies and gentlemen, this very day Germany is preparing a warm, if wet, welcome for your cousins from over the seas—'

'Turn the damned thing off!' Churchill

called angrily, as in the background a military band started to play a very solemn version of the 'Death March' from *Saul*.

Obediently the ancient manservant did as ordered, leaving the echo of that supercilious snarl still circulating in the suddenly silent study. With a wave of his hand Churchill dismissed the servant and now sat alone in the study, listening to the beat of the rain on windows that rattled in a sudden wind. His thoughts weren't pleasant.

He had heard from the Admiralty that the commodore in charge of the convoy was already having trouble with the Americans. Some of them had actually formed a deputation to protest at the pitiful British naval defence of the convoy. Now that the Germans had discovered somehow or other that the convoy's merchant fleet consisted of Yankee ships, as Lord Haw-Haw had just revealed, the Hun would go all out to inflict the greatest possible losses on the merchantmen. Not only would it be a naval victory for the enemy, but it would also be a political one, perhaps even greater than the naval victory. Now it was up to him to try to stave off a possible massacre of the Yankee shipping. Their escorts were of no importance. They were the Royal Navy. As for centuries now the men of the Royal Navy had been trained to die for their country; it was what he and their country expected of them.

But what was he going to do to stave off overwhelming slaughter? God, why had he to make these world-shaking decisions virtually every day that dawned? It was too much. Suddenly the great man broke down. He put his hands up to his face, shoulders shaking, and started to weep like a broken-hearted child...

In contrast, Admiral Doenitz, at his new battle headquarters at Murwick, was happy, or at least as happy as that dour man could be. In the giant operations room, with the naval female auxiliaries climbing up and down the ladders positioned at the huge wall map, while others under the command of elegant young staff officers manned the telephones taking messages from U-boats prowling the world's oceans from Tokyo to Toronto, he gazed happily at his dispositions in the Channel, North Sea and North Atlantic.

The sight gave him pleasure. Everything seemed remote, far distant from the bloody business of actual combat, controlled by a simple command and the shove of a counter depicting a naval craft by means of a long stick.

Speedily Doenitz ran his mind over the day's naval and air dispositions. The Junkers air fleet in Holland had suffered from the convoy's flak barrage; he didn't think he could count on the Luftwaffe at their fields in northern Holland for very effective support until it had replaced its losses. The air fleet in Norway near Oslo was a different matter. It was still intact and not only did its commander have the usual Heinkels and Junkers under command, he had at least two squadrons of Stukas at his disposal. Admittedly the gull-winged dive-bomber was antiquated. But flown by an experienced and brave pilot not afraid to drop out of the sky, using the plane as a target-aimer, it was still an effective and, for the Tommies and their new *Ami* friends, a frightening weapon.

But on this day, with sea mist and overcast skies forecast for the North Atlantic, his E-boats stationed at the Dutch island of Texel would be his best weapons. The wooden craft, which could easily reach forty knots when pushed, would make very difficult targets for the enemy and if they could get within range, their 'tin fish' – their torpedoes – could create havoc within the convoy.

He looked up at his staff. 'Gentlemen, I have made up my mind. This day we shall attack with the Texel E-boat squadron, all six boats of them. We can expect losses, as I can see from the looks on your faces you, too, fear this.' He shrugged his skinny shoulders. 'But as they say, gentlemen, you can't make an omelette without breaking eggs.'

His staff were attentive, but not impressed. They knew Doenitz of old. He felt for his 'blue boys', as he called his sailors, but he expected them to take losses and didn't care overly much how high those losses were.

'Now I want the E-boat squadron to concentrate its attention on this *Ami* ship here.' He indicated with his counter one of the largest of the merchant ships, placed right in the centre of the convoy. 'It is the *Texas Rose*.' He pronounced the name of the US ship with a heavy accent. 'You all know what she carries, of course.'

'Oil, sir,' a senior staff officer answered for the rest. 'That's why she is in the centre of the convoy, to give her as much protection as possible.'

'Exactly, my dear Lohmann.'

'But that also means, sir,' Lohmann objected, 'that the E-boats trying to get close enough to torpedo this, er, *Texas Rose* are going to suffer losses, as you have already pointed out – perhaps grievous ones.'

Doenitz was unmoved by Lohmann's objection. His dark, twisted mind was already full of the moment that he would report to the Führer in Berchtesgaden that the whole *Ami* convoy had been sunk. That would show those old fogies of admirals who had always looked down on the U-boat arm and believed that those tin cans of battle-ships of theirs still had a future, which they hadn't. God, they'd have to look to their laurels if they still attempted to stop his pro-motion. Pull this attack off, he told himself, and he'd be a grand-admiral of the fleet yet. Aloud Doenitz snapped, 'Regardless of losses, Lohmann, we must attack that oil tanker. Perhaps it won't be necessary to sink her. To set her alight might well be suffi-cient. With all that crude oil in her holds she'll burn for hours, perhaps even a day or so, before she sinks. And, gentlemen, you know what purpose she'll serve then?' Doenitz answered his own question. 'She'll be a beacon!'

'For what, sir?' Lohmann asked.

'For my U-boats, Lohmann,' Doenitz cried in triumph, his faded eyes suddenly animated by his fanaticism.

Lohmann couldn't quite repress his gasp. So that was it, he told himself. Doenitz would use the Luftwaffe and the surface craft of the E-boat squadron to break down the enemy's resistance, prepare their ships for the kill like the riders did in the Spanish bullring. Then in would come the glamorous bullfighter to execute the kill, to the applause of the crowd. That was it, Lohmann told himself. Damn the Luftwaffe – fat Hermann's fighter and bomber boys were not going to have the kudos of victory if Doenitz had his way. Nor would the surface ships of Grand Admiral Raeder have them either. Victory had to go to Karl Doenitz and his 'blue boys' of the U-boat arm.

Next moment Doenitz confirmed Lohmann's unpleasant suspicions. 'The first wolfpack has already left Calais under the command of one of my aces, *Kapitanleutnant* Hartung,' Doenitz explained. 'I anticipate them being in position by late afternoon tomorrow. By then air and surface vessels will have attacked and carried out what we want on this *Ami Texas Rose*.' He flashed them a smile of triumph.

'Then, *meine Herren*, my U-boats –' Lohmann noted that *my* U-boats with a feeling of repulsion. It indicated that this had almost become Doenitz's private war, fought for his own greater glory – 'will blast all hell out of the enemy convoy. Believe you me, gentlemen, it will be a great slaughter, one that will go down in the annals of naval warfare...'

Six

Little by little the dawn fog had started to disperse. Now the sky to the east began to flush an ominous blood-red. As the U-boat started to sail out of the Channel up along the protection of the German-held Belgian coast, Hartung's cover vanished slowly and he didn't like it. First there had been the murder of poor old Klausen and the frantic search for a submarine engineer officer. Now his cover had virtually gone and, old hare as he was, Hartung began to worry that his luck had finally run out. He knew that all experienced U-boat skippers felt like this after they had completed half a dozen combat missions – most U-boat crews didn't last more than three missions. Yet it seemed to him that the odds were against him this time.

He had lost his cover and his most skilled officer. Now Doenitz had ordered that he make the best surface speed in order to reach the rendezvous in time. But how long could he remain on the surface where he could achieve a better speed than he could submerged? Once the fog had cleared completely and Tommy's radar, not far away on the other side of the 'pond', picked him up, he'd be 'right up to his hooter in crap', as the ratings described it. Now he started to scan the sky to the west anxiously for the first sign of enemy aircraft, for he knew that in such shallow water, even if he were submerged, any halfblind Tommy pilot would be able to spot him; and once they'd hooked on to him, they'd have half the shitty RAF out over the sea ready to blast him to eternity.

Next to him the lookout focused his huge binoculars and said, 'Sir, U-332 is slowing down – a lot.'

Hartung forgot the Tommies. He flung himself behind the binoculars mounted permanently on the conning tower hatch and stared through the twin circles of glass.

The lookout was right, the U-332 commanded by Lieutnant Barthels, the arch-Nazi, was slowing down. 'What in three devils' name is Barthels doing reducing speed here?' he cursed to no one in particular. Barthels, 'Nazi piss pansy', as loose-mouthed Klausen used to call him, was, despite his fanatical devotion to the creed of National Socialism, an old hare like himself. He knew the dangers of reducing speed in these waters and under these weather conditions, so why was he doing so? Was he having trouble with his diesels perhaps? The new class of bigger U-boat that Barthels commanded had a bad reputation in that area.

Hartung adjusted his glasses more finely, using the enhancer to lighten the image. Now he could make out the dark figures lining each side of the U-332's hull. All of them were holding long boathooks and prodding the water delicately like fishermen trying to pull some wily, tricky trout. 'Great crap on the Christmas tree!' he cursed. *'Mines.'*

Down below the lookout confirmed his reading the next minute, and next to him on the bridge one of the conning tower crew exclaimed, 'Now the tick-tock is really in the pissbucket,' and crossed himself hastily.

Hartung didn't hesitate. He realized immediately what had happened. The minesweepers from Calais had swept the channel free earlier on and once they had vanished, the Tommy fleet air arm of Coastal Command had come zooming in to drop fresh mines in the supposedly mine-free channel. It was an old trick, but a very dangerous one.

Hartung didn't hesitate, though he didn't know exactly what he could do. Bending over the voice tube, he called the engine room and commanded, 'Both ahead – dead slow!'

At five knots his own boat started to approach the U-332. Five minutes later Hartung saw the reason for Leutnant Barthels' slowness. The first deadly black ball, containing half a ton of high explosive, bobbing up and down, its horns almost touching the submarine's hull, was within millimetres of hitting the hull and exploding. Next to him the other bridge lookout said fervently, 'God Almighty, if that goes up...' The rating didn't finish the sentence; he didn't dare.

Five minutes later the two U-boats were within a couple of hundred metres of each other, crawling across the sea, coloured a blood-red from the rising sun. All was tense, nerve-racking expectancy. Guns were manned. Air lookouts had been doubled and every sailor issued with a life-jacket – just in case.

Now the U-332 stopped moving altogether. Barthels was going to do something about the mine that was threatening to bump against the bow and blow him and his crew to extinction at any moment.

Hartung reacted immediately. 'Stop both,' he snapped down the tube. His boat stopped almost immediately, and now he poised on her bridge, head cocked to the faint breeze, trying to pick up the sounds from the U-332. He had ordered immediate radio silence within the wolfpack. He didn't want the Tommies picking up any of their radio signals; that would be suicidal.

On Barthels' boat two hefty sailors, probably sweating despite the coolness of the morning, were exerting all their strength to push the half-ton mine away with their bow-hooks, which were bending under the strain. Hartung knew what Barthels was trying to do. He'd have the mine pushed away as far as the two ratings could manage, then at once he'd have his boat reverse or move forward, depending on which way the mine went. It was a tricky manoeuvre, but Hartung realized it was the only way to do it.

Tensely and in utter silence he and the rest of the bridge watched as the ratings, leaning on the bending boathooks as if they were pole vaulters about to spring upwards, pushed with all their might. Hartung prayed that they would succeed, for he knew he was already too close to the U-332 for safety. Soon he'd have to back off or endanger the U-222, his own boat.

Suddenly, startlingly, Barthels' diesels began to throb once more. The U-332 started to move forward at a snail's pace, hardly a ripple of white water at her bow. The mine was moving! On the bridge of his own boat, Hartung felt a cold trickle of sweat begin to run down his spine unpleasantly. His hands trembled. Would Barthels be able to do it?

The mine was definitely moving away, though every now and again there was a heart-stopping moment when the slight current threatened to wash the evil, spiked monster back against the U-boat's hull. Instinctively Hartung closed his eyes. But the resultant explosion didn't take place. Just in time the two ratings, their singlets black with sweat, managed to push the mine away.

Then finally it was done and as Barthels increased his speed the mine started to bob away in the wave of the U-332. Hartung would have dearly loved to have turned his machine gun on the infernal machine and blown it out of the water, but he knew that was out of the question. The explosion might have exploded another mine, for Hartung suspected they found themselves right in the centre of the Tommy minefield.

Up ahead, Barthels wiped the sweat from his face and breathed out hard. 'Engine room,' he called down the tube, 'half speed.' Raising himself, he cupped his hands and called more loudly to the deck lookouts, 'Keep your eyes peeled on deck ... Don't relax for a min—'

The command died on his lips. About one sea mile away to port, a fiery-red rocket, trailing burning sparks behind it, flashed into the sky. It was followed that same instant by a muted burst of heavy gunfire. Just off the bow, water erupted in a wild white fountain. '*Scheisse!*' Barthels cursed, and automatically threw up his glasses. It was a fatal move. It wasted time. He should have dived immediately. Instead he adjusted the focus of his binoculars in a hasty attempt to identify the source of the gunfire.

Then he had it. Dark shapes slid into the circles of bright glass, white foam leaping up at their bows, their guncrews already poised behind their quick-firers on the forward deck. 'Tommies!' he yelled. 'Great crap on the Christmas tree, Tommy motor torpedo boats!'

To the rear of Barthels' U-boat Hartung didn't wait to identify the surprise attacker. He hit the klaxon in one movement, crying as he did so, 'Bridge watch – down below ... *Dalli... Dalli* ... down below.'

The men needed no urging. Shells were beginning to fall around the wolfpack everywhere. Travelling as they were at some forty knots, the Tommy gunners were still amazingly accurate. It wouldn't be long before one of his pack, probably Barthels' boat, would be hit. But Hartung wasn't waiting to find out. The survival of the majority was of paramount importance now; Barthels would have to sacrifice himself, if necessary, for the rest.

Like an eel, he slipped through the hatch. Hastily he locked the hatch cover of the conning tower and then he was sliding down the steel ladder to the control room in a shower of sea water, yelling orders as he did so. Up above, already crippled by a lucky Tommy shot to his rudder, Barthels prepared to fight to the end.

Five minutes later it happened. As the command U-boat sank lower and lower, and in the sudden blood-red light of the submerged boat, Hartung ordered 'silent running', adding, 'I'll have the eggs off'n anybody who makes unnecessary noise – with a blunt razorblade.'

A petty officer ignored that dread threat, crying, as he lifted the earphones from his shaven skull, *'Sir, they've hit the U-332! ... Torpedo midships!'*

Hartung gasped. 'Is she sinking?'

' 'Fraid so, sir. Her screws are out of the water.'

Hartung, the old hare, knew what that meant. The U-332 was breaking up with her stern out of the sea, her screws churning purposelessly. For a moment he allowed himself the memory of Barthels celebrating at the monthly *Kameradschaft* evenings when they had been in port. Barthels had been a bit of a prig, a typical product of the new system, given to spouting a lot of bull about the superiority of the Aryan race and all that nonsense, but he had been a good officer, caring a great deal for his men, unlike some of the new Nazi officers who had started coming into the service just before the war. Now within minutes he would be dead, if he weren't dead already. For he knew the Barthels of this world. They might be arrogant bores, but they'd fight to the end, wouldn't surrender.

A moment later he had forgotten all about the young U-boat skipper as one of the petty officers at the hydrophones called softly, 'Something off the port side. Listen, sir.'

For an instant Hartung thought he meant that the British motor torpedo boats were launching depth charges at the submerged U-boat, but then he remembered that they didn't carry depth charges normally; their main weapon was the torpedo. This was something else. He strained his ears. Then he heard it. There was no mistaking that metallic scraping sound on the hull. They had knocked into a mine. For one long moment no one reacted. In the eerie red-glow they remained rooted to the spot, transfixed as if for ever, eyes wide and staring with horror.

Hartung reacted. In a hoarse whisper, he ordered, 'Slow – dead slow, engine room.'

The hum of the big electric motors died

away. The U-boat slid slowly and noiselessly through the water. Still that dread sound of the mine rubbing against the hull continued. Hartung found himself beginning to sweat again. He told himself as his heart began to thump as if it might burst out of his breast cage at any moment that all their lives now hung on a very frail thread. The slightest pressure on one of those rotten horns that protruded from all over the mine and that would be that; they'd all be dead in a matter of seconds.

Mentally, while the crew stared at him as if he were the only one who could save them from death, he started to count off the seconds as he calculated how long it would take the mine to run the length of the hull at the speed they were going just now.

'*Five ... six ... seven.*' The U-boat gave a sudden lurch. Hartung jumped visibly. He opened his mouth to say something. Nothing happened. He closed it again, his face glazed in sweat as if he had rubbed it with vaseline. He attempted to wipe the sweat away with a hand that shook visibly. '*Eight... nine ... ten...*'

Abruptly the scraping stopped. For a second or two Hartung couldn't believe his own ears. He strained, head cocked to one side. But it was true. The scraping had stopped.

All around the crew stared at him expectantly, their faces hollowed out to red death's heads in that eerie light. 'Comrades,' he said hoarsely, trying to control his voice, now the pressure was off. 'I think we've done it...' He couldn't contain himself any longer, shoulders bowed, gasping as if he had just run a long race. '*Shipmates*,' he said with heartfelt relief, 'we've done it ... The Tommies won't get us this time. Chief Petty Officer, see that the crew get a bottle of good Beck's beer with their fart soup this evening.'

If the men had been capable of doing so, they would have cheered the skipper at that moment.

Seconds later they were cutting through the water at eight knots, the soft purr of the U-boat's electric motors growing steadily in intensity. Soon they would be in the open sea, out of that terribly dangerous Channel. Once more they had been saved, and as an exhausted Hartung watched his crew, animated by the thought of a beer in an hour's time, go about their duties with renewed hope, he told himself that they had been saved because Providence had a special task for them. The Tommies and their *Ami* allies would have to pay for the death of *Leutnant* Barthels and his crew. The time to strike was getting ever closer.

Book Four

Horror in the North Atlantic

One

In the distance the *Texas Rose* was still burning brightly: a fiery beacon that probably could be seen a dozen miles away, Smythe estimated. Since then two other American freighters had been hit and were sinking slowly, Orr-Jenkins' escorts unable to sink them on account of the survivors, who were still being rescued. Undoubtedly, Smythe, weary, sweat-soaked and filthy from the flying soot from the sinking vessels, told himself the convoy commander would order them, and the tanker, to be torpedoed as soon as everyone was rescued; the ships gave away the convoy's position all too easily; and they were expecting another E-boat attack like the one that had caught them by surprise at noon with such devastating results. By now ten per cent of the US convoy had been sunk, and Bear Island was still a long way off.

Feeling down and not a little exhausted, Smythe watched as a rubber Carley float came drifting by on the mirrorlike sea. In it there was a man. Even without his glasses, the young officer could see the man was dead. The Yank squatted there too stiffly to be still alive, his teeth a gleaming unnatural white against the greasy black mask of his face.

As the *Black Swan* passed the dead man on his float, Smythe forced himself to look down on him: a pitiful relic of the sea, soaked in diesel oil, stone-cold already, swished back and forth by the swell, useless and somehow, the young officer didn't quite know why, disgusting in death. He shivered and was glad when the Carley float began to drift away.

Not that the *Black Swan*'s ratings on the lower deck were moved by the dead man. Perhaps they knew that sooner or later they'd be dead, at the mercy of the cruel, unfeeling sea, as he was. They were busy with the boathooks like noisy fishermen scenting a good catch. They knew how well supplied Yankee ships were. Now they searched the swell for booty, fishing between the flotsam, hoping to pull out a carton of Lucky Strikes or Camels, worth a fortune on

Hull's black market; perhaps even a bottle of Scotch, which they could hide down below and take fly swigs from when the petty officers weren't looking.

'Not a pleasant sight, eh, young snotty.'

Smythe turned, startled. It was Lt Commander Donaldson, looking old, haggard. The day's battle with the German E-boats had been hard on him. Still, he wasn't drunk, though obviously he'd been drinking; his old eyes were gleaming too brightly.

'No, sir,' Smythe agreed.

'Look at them,' Donaldson went on, 'larking about like heartless schoolkids, with apparently nae an ounce o' pity for yon dead seamen.'

Smythe was surprised. He had never heard the dour Scot speak so much in one go before. But he remained silent, wondering why Donaldson was talking to him like a Dutch uncle. Mostly the skipper didn't seem to notice that he even existed.

'But ye must mind, Smythe, that those boys, those HO fellers, boys that they may seem now, will be dead men themselves sooner or later, probably sooner.' Donaldson tugged the end of his red nose as, below, one of the men 'fishing' pulled up a carton of cigarettes and yelled in triumph at his find to his mates. 'If the Jerries don't get them, the sea will. So they play their cruel games while they can. If they didn't, and thought what was going to happen to them before 1942 is out...' Donaldson shrugged and left the rest of his sentence unfinished.

Smythe, as young and innocent as he was, began to realize there was more to Donaldson than he had thought.

The minutes passed leadenly, as the flow of flotsam started to dry up and the seamen down below began to get bored with their attempts to fish up something of value from the sea. Still Donaldson continued to stare down at the grey wash and the remaining sailors with their boathooks as if he could see something known only to him. Smythe, for his part, waited to be dismissed, though at the same time he was curious about what was going on in the skipper's head.

Finally Donaldson turned and looked directly at him, his red-rimmed boozer's eyes very serious. To the north the Aurora Borealis started to flame, its streamers twisting and turning all the time, growing and waning, now colouring the sea an eerie unearthly green and red. 'Ye see, young Smythe, we are all quite insignificant in the order of things. Look at that sky and the sea.

What do we count against that?' It seemed to be a question and Smythe fumbled for an answer, though later he realized that it had been a question to which the skipper had not expected an answer.

'I don't exactly know, sir,' he stuttered.

Donaldson didn't seem to hear. Instead he said, very businesslike now, 'Remember this, Smythe. You're barely out of your teens, a snotty, the lowest creature in the pecking order. But sooner or later, with just me and CPO Tidmus capable of commanding the *Black Swan*, you might have to take charge.'

Smythe felt himself blushing as of old; he was embarrassed that such an old man as the skipper was should be talking to him in this fashion, as man to man in a way. 'Yessir,' he heard himself mumble.

'Then I know you will do your duty.' Donaldson raised a tobacco-stained finger as if in warning. 'But there is duty and duty, Smythe. There is your duty to the service, the Royal Navy, and there is, however, a higher duty, ye ken.' He paused as if he expected the young officer to say something.

Smythe did so. 'What is that, sir?'

'It is to your fellow men, the men under your command, and that is a harder duty to carry out. In my case it ruined me, marked the end of my career. But I don't regret what I did.' And with that he turned to mount to the bridge and take over the con from CPO Tidmus, leaving Smythe perplexed and even a little worried.

The rest of the day passed routinely. The Germans came again. This time from the air. The escort was ready for them, glad the attack was coming from the sky and not from the super-fast E-boats, which seemed to skim across the water and made difficult targets. The attackers were Heinkels instead of the usual Junkers 88s. The pencil bombers, as the sailors called the German machine, with its pencil-slim fuselage, were slower than the Junkers, and, armed as they were with torpedoes weighing two tons each, they were even slower than usual.

Thus it was that the ack-ack gunners of the escort and those of the American merchantmen that were armed welcomed, in a way, the attack from these slow-moving, low-flying bombers as a means of getting their own back for the losses already inflicted on the convoy, especially for the disastrous German attack on the *Texas Rose*, still blazing, away to their rear.

The Heinkels came in bravely enough. Their tactics were simple. One would attack from port, the other from starboard in the hope of putting the gunners below off their mark. This failed, and now, as they came streaking over the surface of the sea in order to launch their torpedoes, the gunners opened up with a will.

Up on the outer fringe of the convoy, Orr Jenkins' command ship took up the challenge first. As the lead Heinkel dropped his torpedo, Orr-Jenkins yelled to the man at the wheel, 'Hard to port, man ... *hard to port.*' Then, with the sweat streaming down his plump face, the commodore swung round on the bridge of his corvette as the banks of 'Chicago pianos', as the crew called the massed .5-inch machine guns, opened up with an ear-splitting roar.

The massive burst of tracer fire caught the Heinkel just at the wrong moment – for the Heinkel. Relieved of its two-ton burden, the pilot started to rise, revealing its blue-painted belly. In a flash the Heinkel's bottom was ripped apart by that massive opening burst of fire. Metal rained down like leaves in an autumn storm. Desperately the pilot tried to keep his plane airborne. To no avail. The starboard engine was already blazing, trailing thick black oily smoke behind it.

The triumphant gunners showed no mercy. They kept blazing away. The plane shredded metal everywhere. Then as the dying plane zoomed over the bridge of the corvette, Orr-Jenkins caught a fleeting glimpse of the pilot slumped dead or unconscious over his controls, the shattered joystick speared through his chest. Next instant the Heinkel hit the water on the other side of his ship and disintegrated.

But he had no time to congratulate himself on his victory. There were more of the buggers coming in from the watery sun, hoping its weak rays might blind the gunners below. They didn't. Carried away by the crazy atavistic bloodlust of battle, they poured on the fire, hitting plane after plane.

On the *Black Swan*, too far away to add their fire to that of the escort, the crew watched and cheered. Even CPO Tidmus, as old as he was, was carried away by the excitement and the youthful energy of the HO ratings. 'Come on, yer buggers!' he yelled in his flat east-coast accent. 'Come on and have a hole punched in yer arse!' Standing next to him on the upper deck, watching the spectacle, Smythe told himself it all seemed like some gigantic bonfire night – with a lethal outcome. The sky was full of flame, white and red tracer zigzagging everywhere in crazy confusion, planes screaming in, trailing smoke behind them, torpedoes cutting the water in a series of bubbles, with the escort twisting and turning, avoiding disaster at the very last moment.

But as the attack started to peter out, with Heinkels trying to make their escape to the east and their bases in Norway, many of them limping along trailing smoke behind them, and the sweating, happy gunners, splashing their red-hot guns with cold water, savouring the hot cocoa that the cooks were rushing from the galleys below, a lone bomber sneaked in from an unexpected direction – from the west.

Later Orr-Jenkins reasoned the pilot must have been one of the few old hands left in a Luftwaffe, its pilots decimated in the battle for Russia. At all events, he had decided not to come in with the usual attack formations. Instead, he had flown out as far west as his fuel tanks had allowed him to and then had turned back eastwards, calculating that the British radar operators would be concentrating on the east and not the west and the vastness of the North Atlantic.

Now, as the survivors were escaping from that tremendous barrage and the gunners were being stood down or busy replenishing their ammunition for another attack, the lone Heinkel had come winging in, now and then cutting off the motors so that its approach was almost noiseless. Then, with a sudden loud snarl, the pilot turned on both engines. The Heinkel sped forward. Below he selected his target. Skilled as he was, he recognized it for what it was.

The *Ami* ship wasn't large, but he knew from his ship recognition tables that it was his best target under the circumstances. The fire-points everywhere on the freighter's upper deck told him that. She was an ammunition ship. One strike and she'd go up in a flash. There'd be no need for another attack; it was something he was banking on.

'Torpedo man,' he called into his throat mike. 'Ready?'

'Ready as I can be, skipper,' the torpedo man, an old hare like himself, replied. 'I'll shove the tin fish up the *Ami*'s arse so far that his glassy orbs'll pop out of their sockets.'

The pilot laughed grimly and answered, 'Well, make sure you do. There'll be champers and as many of those Norwegian blondes as you can fuck if we get away with this one. *'Los!'*

'Los,' the other man yelled back. *Hals und Beinbruch, Herr Leutnant.*★

Bracing himself as the first flak started to erupt below, the pilot thrust the joystick forward, feeling the adrenaline pumping through his veins. The nose of the bomber tipped downwards dramatically. He could feel his face flatten against the facial bones with the pressure of the G-force. He knew he had to keep control, otherwise he might well black out. Down and down the bomber roared, seemingly set on a course of death, bound to plunge deep into the sea, which was looming up ever larger.

But still the old ace kept control. He was already counting off the seconds. Soon he would pull out and come surging in at wave-top height to launch his tin fish. Flak was now pouring upwards. But the Heinkel bore a charmed life. It flashed through the network of brown puffs of smoke that were anti-aircraft shells exploding.

The pilot grunted. It was time to level out. With all his strength, heaving with both hands, the veins standing out like wires in

★Roughly, 'Break your neck and bones', i.e. Happy landings.

his forehead, he started to pull the Heinkel out of that death-defying dive. A moment later he had done and was zooming in, his props lashing the water just below him into a white fury.

Hardly recognizing his own voice, the pilot sobbed and shrieked, 'Fire torpedo!'

The torpedo man needed no urging. He repressed the nausea that threatened to overcome him, his throat full of hot vomit under that tremendous pressure, and pressed the firing button. The Heinkel leaped twenty metres. The torpedo fell from the plane. It hit the water flatly as it should. Next moment in a flurry of exploding bubbles it was running straight and true, heading for the ammunition ship...

Just beyond the horizon *Kapitanleutnant* Hartung waited. Soon the time of decision would arrive.

Two

Through his periscope, Hartung saw the blinding bright flash of light on the horizon and knew immediately that the daring Luftwaffe ploy had worked. The lone Heinkel, piloted by the leading ace of the Russian front, *Staffelkapitan* Heidenreich, had hit its target. Now the exploding ammunition ship, which had replaced the burned-out *Ami* oil tanker as a beacon for his wolfpack, would lead his five remaining U-boats right on to their target.

But as he lowered the periscope to the regulation twelve metres so that it was not visible on the surface, he knew that he shouldn't underestimate the Tommy escort ships. The English had been fighting Doenitz's U-boats since late 1939. The enemy knew all the tricks and they did have an excellent radar system at their disposal, manned by ratings who were experts at their deadly trade.

In the glowing red light, his crew stared at their skipper in tense expectation. All of them, even the dumbest cook, knew that this was the moment of truth. The captain had now to decide how to attack the enemy convoy; and he had to get his plan of attack right from the beginning. Once the engagement commenced, *Kapitanleutnant* Hartung would be unable to change it. That would mean communication between his various U-boats spread over scores of kilometres would soon be picked up by the enemy and used against the wolfpack. So they waited for the captain to make his decision.

He made it. He said, voice subdued and serious, though his hard face revealed none of the tensions that animated him at this moment, for he was well aware that if he had made the wrong decision these young men looking at him in that eerie unreal light might well be dead before the next twenty-four hours were over, 'We and the other boats, comrades, will naturally try to dodge the escorts. As you know they are spread out in a loose circle around their merchantmen, rather like sheepdogs guarding their flocks against wolves.' He laughed shortly, but there was no answering light in his steely

216

blue eyes. 'Well, we are those wolves and we are not about to reveal ourselves and set the dogs off barking so that some damned shepherd can pop us off with his shotgun. No, there has to be another method.'

The crew nodded their agreement, but no one spoke, for now they were going to learn the worst – or the best: the decision that was to influence whether they lived or died.

'Right, comrades, we attempt to go beneath the escort line. Now how do we do that? First by night, and then one of the wolfpack will create a diversion.' Hartung didn't go into the details of what that diversion would be; it was unnecessary. The less his young crew knew about the complications of the attack, the better. 'Once we have four boats through we spread out and surface.'

There was a slight gasp at that. Someone at the rear of the boat exclaimed, 'Heaven, arse and cloudburst – surface right in the middle of an enemy convoy!'

Hartung ignored the comment. He went on. 'With luck it will be just before dawn, with our targets clearly silhouetted against the new light from the east. That will mean we will have a far better chance of hitting them with one tin fish. After all, the number of our torpedoes is limited, comrades.'

Hartung continued, explaining the technicalities of this daring operation and the dangers, emphasizing that once they were through the escort's cordon there would be no further communication between the various members of the wolfpack, and once the operation was successfully concluded it was every boat for itself. Individual skippers would make their own plans. *'Alles klar, Kameraden?'* Hartung ended his briefing with a smile of encouragement.

'Alles klar, Herr K-lo,' his crew replied dutifully, but even as they did so Hartung knew they had their doubts and were not prepared to ask that overwhelming question that plagued him, too: once they had started their attack from within the convoy and the escort ships had tumbled to their presence there, how were they to get out again? For the time being, he told himself, he'd not attempt to answer that particular question.

Now all doubts were forgotten as the young crew prepared for the great attack. The conning tower hatch was opened and the men took turns in gulping the good clear sea air. Soon they were to be breathing the foul air of the submarine, stinking of bilge, oil and the constant farting of men who had to share one lavatory among nearly forty crew members. Torpedoes were checked and re-checked. Ship recognition tables were consulted for the fastest and most important ships they might encounter in the enemy convoy. Engineer artificers went up and down the banked-up sub engines, listening to each one with a cup-like instrument as a doctor might check a patient's heart with his stethoscope. Even the cooks were involved, making a special dish for the men about to go into battle, the sailors' favourite, *Hamburger Labkaus* – 'the condemned man's last supper', as the crew called it with macabre humour.

Then as the light started to fade, Hartung gave his orders. They were brief and to the point. 'To the attack, comrades ... *Es lebe Deutschland!*'

'*Es lebe Deutschland!*' The cry was echoed by a score or more young voices.

Then without any further ado, Hartung nodded to his second-in-command. 'All right, she's yours.'

The U-boat shuddered as the electric motors started up once more and the lean grey craft surged through the water, heading for the battle to come and her unsuspecting victims...

The *Black Swan* moved slowly through the wreckage of the US ammunition ship. It was growing dark rapidly, but Orr-Jenkins still hoped to find survivors before the light went altogether. As he had signalled Donaldson, 'See if you can find any of the poor buggers. They won't last much longer as it is. But they certainly won't survive the night. The water's freezing. Good luck.'

So far they had found two, bobbing up and down in the water weakly, their faces black with oil, their eyes wide and staring like those Smythe remembered from seaside minstrel shows of his childhood. One had died even as a rating had got a rope round him to pull him out of the sea, so Donaldson personally had gone over the side to haul the second one out of the water, crying over his shoulder as he did, 'Hot grog and plenty of blankets.' Above him CPO Tidmus had added his voice to that of the skipper, snapping, 'Come on, you HO men, look bloody lively.'

Five or ten minutes later they had come to the third and last survivor of the sunken ammunition ship. He was a small fat man, shivering like a drenched dog, blood streaming from a nasty gash on his forehead down the oil-black surface of his chubby face. The fat man hadn't the strength to haul himself up the rope ladder swaying back and forth in the waves, so Hawkins, the strongest man on board, a giant of a man from Devon, reached down to grab hold of the fat American's hands.

The fat man screamed piteously. He fell back in the water, unconscious at once, leaving a horrified Hawkins to stare down at the two fistfuls of charred flesh he had just pulled off the Yank. They looked like a pair of black gloves. Hawkins choked and started to vomit.

Donaldson had had enough. 'All right,' he ordered, 'break off the search. It's getting dark. We'd better get back to our old position.'

Smythe, like the rest of the crew, was only too glad to cease searching for the survivors of the sunken ammo ship. He had seen enough horrors this day to last him a lifetime. As he told CPO Tidmus, the old man's face grey and haggard and ill-looking, while they sipped a cup of cocoa at the bow, 'I never thought it was going to be as bad as this, Chiefie. How do the men stand it, convoy after convoy, I wonder?'

'They don't, sir, that's the short answer.'

Tidmus hesitated a moment, savouring the warmth of the steam rising from the cup. 'Sooner or later they become victims themselves.' He hesitated. 'Or they go barmy, go on the trot and end in the glasshouse, sir.' He took a sip of his cocoa and they were silent for a moment, each man wrapped in a cocoon of his own sombre thoughts.

Down below a dead man floated by. By the look of his grey head he had been oldish. No one would pick him up now. He would float like this for days until he finally sank into oblivion for good. Who would remember him? All his shipmates, who had served with him in rusty old tubs during the Depression, got drunk with him on cheap rum in South American dives and who had come here to the cold Atlantic to die, would be dead, too, this time.

CPO Tidmus broke the heavy silence. 'That poor bugger's had his cards stamped for good, sir,' he remarked, as if talking about the weather and not a human being whose existence had been stamped out so dramatically, so violently.

Smythe couldn't help himself. He shivered violently. But as always the old petty officer saved him from embarrassment. He said, finishing his cocoa, Aye, sir, it's getting right parky now. Best we go below and get warmed up, sir, before we turn in. For all yer know, we might not get much kip this night.'

'Yes, you're right, Chiefie,' Smythe agreed hastily, eager to get away from the sight of the dead American seaman, his grey head lolling from side to side in the swell like that of a broken doll. But he knew he wouldn't sleep so easily this night; he had seen too much. The horrors wouldn't let him rest. But young Smythe was wrong. Horrors or not, he was asleep heavily within minutes of hitting the crumpled, dirty bunk in his little cabin.

Unlike the youth, CPO Tidmus didn't sleep. He told himself he didn't need much kip, despite the strain on his skinny old body. Instead, he did what he always did. He toured the crew's quarters, checking and reassuring. He could see that those who still remained on their feet in the fetid atmosphere of the lower deck were very tired. Their eyes were bloodshot, their faces were haggard and dirty; most of them were unshaven, too.

Tidmus wasn't surprised. In the ablutions their flannels were as hard as boards, the soap frozen in the dirty scum of the water-filled zinc washbasins. At the best of times, once they were at sea, most of the matelots confined themselves to a cat's lick, save for brave souls who stripped naked and washed in the bowls of ice-cold water. Now they had an excuse not to wash properly. By the time they reached Bear Island they'd be stinking to high heaven, many of them coming out with spots and sores due to their dirtiness.

Outside in the little separate room they used as a makeshift sick bay the Yank they had successfully pulled out was moaning, despite the morphia the skipper had pumped into him after giving his wounds a makeshift kind of treatment, taking his instructions from the dogeared ship's medical handbook. With a bit of luck he might last till Bear Island, where he'd get proper attention. If he didn't ... Tidmus shrugged and didn't think that particular thought to its end.

He'd experienced days at sea like this before. They passed but it seemed they were never-ending. For a moment his nerve broke. He shouted at Hawkins, who was now fiddling nervously with his precious personal radio. 'For Chrissake, Hawkins, turn it on! Get any bloody thing. Even that frigging *ITMA* of yours.'

Hawkins obliged, twirling the dial.

So it was they sailed on to the sounds of Tommy Handley's 'Mayor of Foaming-at-the-Mouth' chattering his nonsense to a crew of exhausted young men who might well he dead by the morning...

Three

The big Yank, whom they had rescued first, died, surprisingly enough, while the other much worse injured survivors of the US ammo ship continued to live, even the one that Donaldson had pumped full of dope to ease the pain of dying.

Donaldson, with the aid of Smythe, had been trying to sew on the half-severed ear of an American who was apparently a cook and who had been burned severely by an over-turned pan of cooking oil about the genitals. He whimpered as the curved carpenter's needle went through his ear, his hands held protectively over his red-raw genitals. It had been about then that the Yank they thought they had saved began his crazy ranting.

'Goddamn bastards of Limeys ... fucked

up Limeys ... why did we ever get into the war to save your fucking empire? Can't even fight your way out of a frigging paper bag...' On and on the enraged Yank, his face a crimson-red, ranted, eyes staring straight ahead at some sight known only to him; it was as if he didn't even know he was surrounded by Britishers trying to help the American survivors the best they could with the primitive instruments available to them. Why he ranted thus, they did not know. Nor had they the time to attempt to pacify the Yank. It was as if he thought America's new allies were his country's worst enemies. 'God Almighty, why did we ever get together with the Limeys? ... Lindberg and the America Firsters were right.' Froth was now forming in the big Yank's lips, as if he were going mad.

Smythe looked at him in horror. Who Lindbergh and the America firsters were, he hadn't the faintest idea, and he knew he daren't ask Donaldson, who was cursing fluently under his breath as the bloody cook's ear kept slipping out of his grasp. But the big Yank and his crazy rantings frightened him more than the sight of the fat cook's scalded, red-raw genitals, which were now beginning to swell alarmingly and come

226

out in a rash of white spots, filled with pus.

In the end he was glad when the big Yank abruptly sat bolt upright and cried, 'The damned motherfuckers,' and then next instant slumped to the bloody, littered deck, dead before he hit it.

Later as he watched with CPO Tidmus the sailmaker sew up the dead Yank in a canvas cover and then, just before he covered the face, thrust his curved needle through the Yank's tongue, as was the old naval custom, to test whether he was really dead, he asked, 'Why do they hate us so much, Chiefie?'

Tidmus, looking older than ever, knew who the young officer meant. 'The Yanks?' He shrugged his skinny shoulders. 'God knows! Perhaps on account of the fact that they were once part of the British Empire and had to fight us to start their own country ... Perhaps because the English stock of the old days has worn out and been replaced by Eyeties, Jerries and the like, sir.' He pulled a face. 'But one thing is for certain, they're going to be the new bosses. One day – and one day soon – they'll be telling us what to do and not the other way around.'

Smythe looked at the other man in disbelief. 'Go on, Chiefie, pull the other one! I know America's a big country, but we've got our empire, all that red on the map. A third of the world, they taught us at school. They'll never be able to tell us what to do as long as we've got an empire. Mr Churchill wouldn't let 'em—' He stopped short. CPO Tidmus had clicked awkwardly to attention. The carpenter was beginning to shove the weighted body of the dead Yank over the side without any further ceremony.

Smythe clicked to attention, too, and raised his hand to the peak of his cap in salute, as naval custom demanded. Next to him a solemn Tidmus said, 'Poor sod. Don't even know his name and not a prayer said over him.'

Smythe said nothing, but he thought how Tidmus and his kind were strange creatures. A few minutes before the dead Yank, now disappearing beneath the waves, had been cursing his country, England, up-and-down-dale. Yet Tidmus and the rest bore no rancour. The Yank had died a lonely sea-man's death, already borne away by the sea, and they respected him on that count. Very strange! In years to come he would often recall the incident of the dead Yank and tell himself that though English people often had strong prejudices they were not overly touchy about insults to their own country;

perhaps it was indicative of a people who had outgrown nationalism and cheap patriotism. Whether that was good or bad he was never able to work out.

Some time that night, Donaldson called the crew together, even those who were off duty and were 'hot-bedding' – sleeping in the warm smelly hammocks of the ratings who had just gone on watch. The men grumbled at being awakened, but they realized that the skipper's address had to be of some importance, otherwise he would have let them sleep, for all of them were approaching near exhaustion from the strain of the last few days since they had left Hull. Donaldson didn't waste any time, as they stood at ease on the lower deck in the cold spectral light of a sickle moon. 'Tomorrow, men, we'll reach Bear Island, where we'll be a bit safer from enemy attacks. Perhaps even the Russkis'll turn out and give us some extra protection, but I've been told by Chiefie Tidmus here that's hardly likely.'

He allowed them a minute or two to absorb the information before continuing with, 'Half an hour ago I received a signal from the commodore in charge of our convoy that we can expect a submarine attack before dawn. The boys at the top have picked up the enemy signals.' He raised his hand as if to stop any protest. In the event, none came and he went on. 'However, before anyone fills his bell-bottoms, there's a bit of good news. It's this.' He paused and they waited expectantly, silent ghosts in that glowing silver light that illuminated the ships spread out all about them.

'Commodore Orr-Jenkins also signalled that Mr Churchill himself has become aware of our problem. He is sending an aircraft carrier from Scapa Flow *now* to give us support. Before dawn, according to Commodore Orr-Jenkins, the first flight of Sea Hurricanes will be taking off from her and should reach us by first light. I know it will be a matter of nip-and-tuck, but if luck is on our side they'll beat the subs. Once the Jerries have been engaged, the Sea Hurricanes will be followed by the Swordfish carrying depth charges and torpedoes. They'll see off the U-boats for good, once the Hurricanes have them under control—'

'Good old Winnie,' the somewhat effeminate sailor who had asked for permission to grow a beard in what now seemed another age began. But Donaldson cut him short. 'Don't let us count our chickens before they hatch, men,' he snapped. 'The Jerries are cunning buggers and there are a lot of other factors that could upset the apple cart, as far as we're concerned.'

His tone changed. 'One other thing before I dismiss the parade. Commodore Orr-Jenkins signalled something else, concerning the *Black Swan*. He signalled he's going to take a chance that we won't run into mines before we reach Bear Island.' Donaldson hesitated momentarily before adding, 'So to add strength to the escort, we shall be taken off mine-clearing duties at the van of the convoy for the time being. Instead we shall sail in the tail-end Charlie position.'

Hastily Smythe whispered to CPO Tidmus standing next to him. 'Tail-end Charlie? I thought that was the rear gunner in the RAF. What's it mean in the Royal Navy, Chiefie?'

'Same thing in a way. Our tail-end Charlie brings up the stragglers and keeps a weather eye open for any Jerry bugger try to slip us a fly one from the rear.'

Smythe nodded his understanding and listened as Donaldson continued. 'It's not the most enviable position, as the actress said to the bishop.' No one laughed at the skipper's attempt at humour. The crew was too busy considering what new dangers the tail-end position might entail.

'But it's a vital one, men. We can assume the squareheads are trying to catch up with the convoy at this very moment. If they get within firing range, naturally they'll try to sink one of us to slow the whole convoy down. That could be fatal, especially as Met expects good clear skies tomorrow and we could be sitting ducks in such weather conditions. So we've got to keep our eyes skinned and ensure that the squareheads don't get that close until the flyboys get on to them and deal with the buggers once and for all. All right, that's it, men.'

CPO Tidmus opened his mouth to dismiss the parade in correct Royal Navy fashion, but Donaldson stopped him before he could do so. 'No bullshit, Chiefie. Get the off-duty men back to their hammocks. You on-duty chaps, off to your watch.'

'What do you think, Chiefie?' Smythe asked as they walked back through cold silver light to their tiny cabins. 'They say lower-deck people are not paid to think, sir. That's to be left to officers and gents.' There was no criticism in the old petty officer's remark, Smythe knew that. Still, he realized that the older man had thought over Donaldson's final point and had given the matter the consideration of his considerable experience. 'All I can say, sir, it won't be as easy as Commodore Orr-Jenkins and the captain think.'

'Why?'

'Because, sir, some smart U-boat captain'll know what our job is – to warn the convoy ahead of us. So what'll he do?' Tidmus answered his own question. 'He'll consider his first objective will be to get shut of the poor old *Mucky Duck*. Yessir, if anybody's for the chop before this day's out, it'll be yours truly. Good night, sir. I won't wish you pleasant dreams.' And, with that, the old petty officer was gone, leaving the young officer to his thoughts, and they weren't pleasant.

Some ten miles away from the convoy now, Hartung prepared for what was to come. He used the captain's privilege of having a bucket of hot water brought from the galley, placed on the floor behind the drawn curtain while he stripped naked. He knew it was a waste of precious water – most of the crew had already grown beards and, to judge by their stink, hadn't washed for several days now. Hartung was different. He didn't find the customary U-boat man's beard attractive and he certainly detested the stink. If he was going to die in battle, he was going to do so clean.

As he washed himself carefully, not wasting a drop of water, he told himself, as was his custom when he went into battle, he wouldn't eat anything. If he received a wound in his guts he didn't want the shit to infect the wound, because he had always reasoned it'd take an age before he saw a medic, and before then the poison would have set in. Whatever the outcome of the coming battle – and the war – he'd rather end it dead than as a cripple.

Then Hartung forgot his personal problems, and, as he shaved very carefully balancing himself against the motion of the U-boat, he considered what was to come. Four of his wolfpack would penetrate the outer defensive circle of the escorts. The method he'd use had always proved pretty foolproof. He – and the others – would close up to the nearest merchantman and match her speed, hoping that the enemy hydrophone operators listening for the tell-tale noise of the submarine below the surface of the sea might confuse the sound made by his screws with that of the merchantman.

To assist the manoeuvre, he had instructed

his youngest skipper, Jensen, known in the U-Boot arm as the 'Train Buster' (for so far the young skipper had achieved only one 'kill'; he'd torpedoed a Tommy train running along the Egyptian coast), to feint an attack on one of the escort ships. He'd selected a small armed trawler, sailing to the rear of the circle of escorts and ordered Jensen to make a 'run' at it. If Jensen sank it, all well and good; it didn't matter. His main task was to alert the Tommies that there were U-boats to their rear, while the rest of the wolfpack slipped – hopefully – into the centre of the enemy shipping. As he had signalled Jensen, who was obviously not well pleased with his mission, 'Remember, old house, this is no train.' To which Jensen had replied with a suggestion that he ought to do something to himself that was anatomically impossible.

Now *Kapitanleutnant* Horst Hartung was almost ready. He dressed again, feeling good and fresh. As an afterthought he dabbed some cologne on his freshly shaven face. The smell of cologne would arouse some ribald comment from his crew, especially from the old hares, who were no respecters of persons. It didn't worry him. He knew they thought him a very capable person; not a glory hunter like so many of the U-boat skippers, who would risk their crews' lives in order to achieve a piece of cheap tin.*

'Tin,' he said aloud, remembering his own decorations, and he had a drawer full of the cheap baubles. He went over to the little table, the cabin's only furniture apart from an equally small stool and bunk, and opened it to take out the only decoration that meant anything to him.

Carefully he took out his Knight's Cross with Oak Leaves, smoothed out the crease in the black and white ribbon and fastened the highest decoration ever awarded to any sailor of the U-Boat arm around his neck. Thus attired, he drew back the curtain and pushed his way into the cramped evil-smelling corridor to the accompaniment of the admiring whistles of his men. *Kapitan-leutnant* Horst Hartung was ready to do battle.

*Sailors' slang for decorations for bravery.

Four

Jensen knew the plan had gone wrong immediately. Coming straight out of the dawn mist was what looked like an armed merchantman, though smaller. But it was definitely the kind of vessel that Hartung had ordered him to sink: unsuspecting and easy meat. This one was sailing into battle and it already had its opponent in its sights: his U-boat.

He sprang into action, and pushed the alert button. Hoarse klaxons sounded their urgent warning. As the bridge watch scrambled to get below, he hit the chest mike and yelled, 'Skipper ... emergency ... emergency ... DIVE ... DIVE ... DIVE!'

As the alarm bells started to sound in ear-splitting, frightening fury below, he slid down the ladder from the conning tower after the rest to land on all fours in a spray of icy seawater on the deck. Even as he landed, he was snapping out orders, knowing that every second was precious now, meant the difference between life and death.

His men knew it too. As the red under-water lighting sprang on the combat watch hurried to their battle stations; they obeyed the order 'flood' at record time. The water began to pour in, gurgling and boiling, as the engineer glued his gaze to the flood tables, counting off the diving tanks as they filled up, *'Five ... four ... three ... two ... BOTH!'*

Now the sweating ratings, eyes wild and white with tension and not a little fear, opened the valve levers. The bow of the U-boat began to tilt. She started to dive. Now the whole submarine trembled and shivered like a wild thing. The electric motors took over and began to race all out. Next to Jensen the hydrophone operator, slipping off one earphone, yelled, 'Screws almost on top of us, sir.' That would be the enemy ship. Jensen yelled something back. He knew not what.

Next instant he called, 'Thirty-five-degree load!...' This was followed by, 'Down to fifty fathoms.' The strain was all too obvious on Jensen's face, as he pushed his battered cap back to front and prepared to have a quick look through the periscope. He didn't get a chance. The U-boat reeled wildly as something slammed into her hull. Men slithered from one end of the boat to the other. Rivets burst everywhere. Glass instruments followed. Water began to trickle in. Just in time Jensen caught a stanchion and stopped himself falling. They had been hit all right, but the U-boat was still moving. He breathed a quick sigh of relief. 'Silent running,' he ordered, wondering at the calmness of his voice.

All talk ceased. The men hunched there in apprehension. If their attacker carried depth charges, they'd be falling all around the damaged sub in an instant. Jensen caught himself holding his breath like an amateur boxer might do when he expected his opponent to punch him in the guts. The seconds passed in leaden silence. Now they could hear the screws of the enemy ship thrashing away directly above them. It was now or never. In that eerie light their faces, lathered in greasy sweat, were unreal red skulls. Some of the younger ratings were gasping as if they were running out of air, their ribs going in and out hectically under their dirty singlets.

And then it was over. The sound of the enemy's screws started to diminish. The

Tommy must have lacked torpedoes. Jensen forced a smile. The crew began to relax. An old petty officer farted. Someone laughed at the sound. Jensen relaxed his grip on the stanchion near the periscope and wiped the sweat from his young brow. He knew it was a sign of weakness. The crew would know he'd sweated because he had been afraid as they had. But he couldn't help it.

'Close call, comrades,' he said. 'But the Tommies'll have to get up earlier than that, if they want to sink old Train Buster.' He used his unfortunate nickname deliberately. It'd cheer the crew up a bit to know he could poke fun at himself. Then he started to concentrate on the new situation.

Without being told so by the chief engineer, he knew instinctively that the U-boat had been damaged when the Tommy, coming out of the blue, had tried to ram her. How serious the damage was he could only guess, but he did know that his boat wasn't running as well as she should, even though her electric motors were going all out at full power. She was at least a couple of knots slower than she should be.

He frowned. For all he knew he might have difficulty in getting her back to port, but he'd worry about that later. It all seemed part and parcel of the jinx that had plagued him ever since he had been given command of his own U-boat.

He dismissed his current worries. Now he was determined to carry out the mission given to him by Hartung. He'd sink a decoy and then break off the action immediately and head for the nearest Norwegian port. He guessed that by then the enemy convoy would be too busy with Hartung's attack to concern itself with him, especially as he would already have cleared off out of the convoy's area of operations and responsibilities.

He forced a bigger smile and turned once more to his waiting crew. 'Fe, fi, fo, fum,' he quoted in accented English, 'I smell the blood of an Englishman.' He snorted loudly through his nose, as if he really could do so. The crew, even those who didn't understand English, laughed at the captain's saying and facial expression. 'All right, men, we're going to risk it... We're going up.' His smile vanished 'Take her up, Number One ... To periscope height.'

Tensely he waited till his order had been carried out, praying that the boat would rise. She did so, though more slowly than normal. But she was keeping an even keel and the waiting artificers, hammers already poised to seal up any leak, reported one by one that on the whole the plates were holding, even if they had been buckled here and there.

The ascent stopped at the regulation twelve metres below the surface. 'Up periscope,' he ordered.

The crew tensed instinctively, all eyes on the captain. They knew that if the Tommy ship which had tried to ram them was still waiting for them up there, in an instant's time all hell would break loose.

'Stand by gun crew,' the young skipper ordered, as twisting his battered cap round so the peak was to the back of his head, he bent and raised the 'scope from the deck, letting it slide almost noiselessly upwards. He stopped it immediately it broke the surface. For a moment or two he could make out nothing but the wavelets rippling around the glass of the periscope. He edged up a little further, noting as he did so he was breathing faster with tension.

Now the periscope broke the surface cleanly. Immediately he swung it round in a three hundred and sixty arc. The warship that had attacked him on the surface had vanished. In its place there was a fat merchantman, moving at a snail's pace and steadily falling behind the rest of the convoy. He whistled softly. Just the kind of a target that U-boat skippers prayed for.

He made his decision. He couldn't let Hartung and the rest of his fellow U-boat commanders down; he had drawn the escort's attention away from the attempt of the wolfpack to penetrate the convoy. He mustn't miss sinking the slow freighter, and to make perfectly sure that he didn't, he'd have to surface. But that involved risk to his own boat. He turned to the crew. 'We've got a target,' he announced. 'Tubes one to four ready for surface fire.'

The crew didn't hesitate, though now they knew he was going to attack their objective on the surface, with all the inherent dangers of such an attempt. They set about their various duties with practised ease, as if this was just another one of the usual training expercises.

The skipper nodded his approval before commanding, 'All right, take her up.'

A couple of moments later, the conning tower of the U-boat broke the surface. Followed by the conning tower watch, Jensen scrambled into the tower, binoculars raised at once, scanning the horizon once more for an enemy warship. Nothing. Now there was no time to waste. 'Ready down below,' he called over the speaking tube. 'Target Red 90 ... speed eight knots ... range twelve hundred metres...'

He waited. Not for long. From below the ensign at the attack table yelled back, 'Lined up!' referring to their target.

He flung up his glasses once more and surveyed the unsuspecting merchantman as it sailed silently across the glass of the binoculars. For a moment, he wondered about her crew, his unsuspecting fellow human beings and seafaring men, whom he would kill so suddenly in a few moments. Shaking his head, he drove the thought away. It didn't do to think such thoughts in this year of 1942. This year it was kill or be killed. Here it was the law of the jungle and the survival of the strongest.

'Commander to torpedo officer,' he called with sudden harshness. 'Stand by to fire.'

'Tubes one, two, three and four ready to fire, sir.'

'Commander to torpedo officer. Fire when ready.'

'Ready.' Behind the young officer, one of his petty officers was checking off the torpedoes, calling his decisions through the length of the tense hull. 'On ... *on* ... *on*,' indicating that each of the torpedo settings was correct. '*On!*'

The young torpedo officer waited no longer. He knew that every second their U-boat lay on the surface, barely moving, increased the danger for her.

'*FIRE!*' he yelled, his young voice breaking with the tremendous excitement of this moment.

A hiss of compressed air escaping. A wild flurry of bubbles at the boat's bow. A hefty lurch as one after another the torpedoes left the U-boat. Then the torpedoes were streaking for the target, racing in to kill.

On the conning tower the skipper adjusted his binoculars frantically. Around him the rest of the watch did the same. They were animated now by the bloodlust of the hunt, hearts pounding as they waited for that first impact. Below in the boat the crew fell silent. Not a sound could be heard save for the soft throb of the diesels. Only the radioman moved. He fiddled carefully with his dials. Urgently he was trying to pick up any signal the merchantman might make the moment it was hit.

Next to the skipper, a member of the conning tower crew counted off the seconds by means of his stopwatch. The longer he did so, the more likely the fan of torpedoes had missed and overshot their target. But they hadn't. Suddenly – startlingly – a tremendous bang. The men on the bridge reeled back. It was as if a giant damp hand had slapped them across the face. Instinctively they all opened their mouths, looking like a lot of gaping idiots as they did so, in order to prevent their eardrums from being burst by the terrific explosions. Someone yelled, 'Hit aft! We've got the Tommy, comrades ... *WE'VE GOT HER, ALL RIGHT!'*

Five

Hastily Donaldson put the bottle of whisky down, as CPO Tidmus came on to the bridge to report. He had a look of guilt on his face. Tidmus could see that and he knew why. The captain had already heard the explosion and realized what it was. 'Just wanted to report, sir, that one of the Yankees has been torpedoed. Sparks picked up their S.O.S. They seem to have things under control, sir, though I don't know what Commodore Orr-Jenkins is going to think—'

'Commodore Orr-Jenkins can go and fuck himself as far as I'm concerned,' Donaldson cut him off crudely. 'You've got to make sacrifices if you're going to beat yon square-heads. Orr-Jenkins ought to know that. He's been in the service long enough.'

'Yessir,' CPO Tidmus answered dutifully. 'But the Yanks are not going to like it.'

'Then let them lump it, Chiefie. I'm not fighting this war for America, I'm fighting it for my own homeland – Britain.' Now not caring what the wrinkled old petty officer thought of him, Donaldson picked up the bottle of whisky again and took a hefty swig straight from the neck. He coughed throatily, his pale face suddenly a brick-red, and wiped the back of his hand across his wet lips.

Tidmus looked worried. He knew and the captain knew too that Donaldson was in trouble, a great deal of trouble. He had disobeyed Orr-Jenkins' order and that would mean a court of inquiry. These days with so many skippers, naval and merchant navy, turning tail and running away from the frightening dangers of the Murmansk Run, it wouldn't take some bastard on the prosecution team at any inquiry to make out that Donaldson had shown the white feather and had abandoned his post because he had been afraid.

'Chiefie.' Donaldson seemed calmer when he spoke again – perhaps the strong spirits were having an effect. 'I know what I see as my duty and as captain of this old tub *I* decide what she does and does not do.'

'Yessir, I understand that. But what about the powers that be? They might see it differently.'

'Let 'em. I've done this before and I have been punished for having gone it alone. Their Lordships didn't scare me then and they won't scare me now. The point is that I do the max damage to the enemy. That's what this war is about – and the safety of the men under my command.'

'Yessir.'

'I thought when I rammed that Jerry U-boat that I'd sunk her and that was that. But I didn't and I was wrong, as badly wrong as I was in North Africa last year when we ran aground.' He paused and took another swig straight from the bottle, almost defiantly this time.

Just about to enter with the latest signal picked up by Sparks from the sinking US merchantman, Smythe paused. He hadn't heard the skipper's words but he could tell by the look on his face and his drinking straight from the Scotch bottle that there was something seriously wrong. He wondered whether he should go in and then decided he shouldn't. Still, he remained there and listened.

'Chiefie,' Donaldson continued, slurring his words pretty badly now, 'when we ran aground just west of Algiers, and the Frogs trapped us, I should have let it happen. Sooner or later the striped-pants buggers from the Foreign Office would have arranged an exchange for us with their own people we'd just captured in Syria. But I knew all about Mers-el-Kebir in 1940,* how we'd killed a thousand of their sailors and destroyed their fleet, and I'd heard how the Frogs treated our matelots who fell into their hands. The Frogs were worse than

*In 1940 Churchill had ordered the French Navy to be destroyed to stop it falling into German hands. The worst incident happened at the North African port of Mers-el-Kebir where 1,000 French sailors who had been Britain's allies only weeks before had been killed by the Royal Navy.

the Jerries with the Jews; they treated our people like slaves, especially if they were sailors of the Royal Navy.' He shook his head, face set in a look of absolute drunken despair. 'I couldn't let that happen to my boys, could I, Chiefie, could I?'

CPO Tidmus shook his head, a look of pity on his face. Commander Donaldson, as hard as he was, was, he realized, almost at the end of his tether, at breaking point. Now the knowledge that he had allowed one of the Yankee ships to be torpedoed was about the final straw.

'So I engaged the Frogs and fought them off until our ammo ran out and we had to surrender,' Donaldson went on, broken-voiced. 'The casualties were appalling – I'll never forgive myself for losing so many men, but I had to try.' He got a grip on himself. I had to try. Naturally their Lordships never forgave me. I should have shown better judgement and all that sort of thing. The French would have released us in due course, once we got a neutral intermediary working on them. Of course, they did, what was left of the poor buggers, and most of the survivors are in TB hospitals up and down the country today, wrecked men, who'll never go to sea again—' He stopped abruptly and wrung his hands like a man who didn't understand the world any more.

CPO Tidmus took a step forward. 'Now, sir,' he began, but stopped short. The captain was already drinking straight from the bottle once more, and so Smythe left them, unnoticed, like two characters at the end of some cheap melodrama. Yet he was moved beyond comprehension. He had never imagined such things happening in the Senior Service. Dartmouth had never prepared him for such scenes. But now he realized what Donaldson had meant earlier on about a higher duty, a duty to one's crew, even if it wrecked your career.

Still, he knew instinctively he hadn't the guts to do what Commander Donaldson had done, even if he had been older and more experienced. He was fated to be a mere subordinate, who carried out orders without protest, suppressing any private feelings. Feeling a little sick and depressed, he trailed back to Sparks' radio shack, mind heavy with what he had just heard, realizing abruptly that he was growing up much too soon...

Train Buster, some ten miles away, was equally depressed by what he saw as the battered U-boat limped along, past the sinking merchantman. He had finally achieved his first kill as a U-boat commander, but it didn't please him particularly. For now he had the problem of getting back to the safety of the Norwegian coast and the weather was getting worse. The wind was coming from the east. It was bitter and freezing, scudding in straight from the ice cap. Soon, he knew from experience, it would be turning everything before it a sparkling white. And that could only add to the burden of trying to get the U-boat to safety, especially as he didn't dare risk diving any more and would have to stay on the surface. Already the spray and spindrift washing over the hull of his boat was freezing everything and spreading a film of bright hoar frost over the steel casing.

Still, there was little he could do about it, he told himself, and tried not to look over at the still burning merchantman and the panicked sailors who were now flinging themselves over the side in order to escape death by fire only to die within minutes of hitting the freezing water. That might well be his and his crew's fate and he didn't want to be reminded of it.

He snapped an order to the engineer below, commanding him to try to get more speed out of the diesels, though he knew that it was the damage to the hull that was slowing him down and there was nothing he could do about that at the moment. Then he ordered the gun crews up on deck. They were to check the Oerlikon and the machine guns to ensure that they had not already frozen up. At the same time they were to smear the sights with the special winter oil that prevented them from clouding up at a critical moment. Finally he ordered double lookouts to take up their posts at bow and stern. If the Tommies had tumbled to the fact that he had survived the ramming, they might well have their big cumbersome Sunderland flying boats in the general area, which could attack him. The thought didn't worry him particularly. All the same, he had to take all possible precautions. It was still well over a hundred kilometres to the safety of the Norwegian coast. Till then he'd have to maintain radio silence in order not to give his position away to any buck-toothed Tommy listening for enemy signals. Slowly, everything possible that could be done, having been done, the young U-boat skipper started to calm down and concentrate on the task of saving the boat.

Time passed slowly. Behind them the freighter started to disappear. It was still burning, but on the conning tower they could no longer hear the crackle of the flames or – something for which the Train Buster was profoundly thankful – the screams of the men who had flung themselves into the sea and were crying out in their death agonies. Indeed he received some good news which improved his mood somewhat. One of the younger petty officers, who would, the skipper promised himself, receive the Iron Cross, Second Class for his bravery, had volunteered to go over the side to check the damage to the hull at the U-boat's bow. How he had survived immersion in that bone-chilling water for nearly three minutes, the U-boat commander couldn't imagine. But he had. Then he had reported to the captain, trembling like a leaf, hardly able to hold the mug of steaming hot grog someone had thrust into his hand, that the damage wasn't as bad as they had thought. The plates were badly buckled where the U-boat had been rammed. But with the aid of a 'patch'* on the inside of the

*A makeshift measure, comprising wood, sailcloth and metal, used to patch up a hole in a submarine's hull until more comprehensive repairs can be undertaken.

254

hull, she wouldn't ship any more water.

Now Train Buster made his decision. He'd put a double watch on the patch. They'd be ordered to work flat out to repair the great rent in the U-boat's hull. In the meantime, he'd try to coax as much speed from the damaged craft as he could without sinking her. For it seemed to the young U-boat skipper, his face black with the oil from the damaged diesel motors he had inspected earlier on, that soon there would be trouble – lots of trouble in the immediate sea area of the convoy. Once the wolfpack leader got into position – and he knew that old hare Hartung would make it with his bold plan to infiltrate to the centre of the *Ami* convoy – all hell would be let loose and he didn't want to be there when it happened. No sir!

With a defiant grin on his dirty face Jensen turned to the north, braving the icy spray that lashed the conning tower, already turning it a bright gleaming white with frost, and raised his hand in salute. 'For those who are about to die, O Caesar,' he intoned solemnly, 'we salute thee!'

An instant later his solemn tone vanished and he added in his normal tone, 'Best of luck, you lucky arsehole, Hartung. Sink any Tommy and *Ami* bastard that comes into your sights.' Now, the wolfpack leader, somewhere in the deep below the convoy, forgotten, concentrated on the self-imposed task of getting his damaged U-boat back to some safe harbour on the coast of Norway.

He never made it. Within sight of Bergen, the U-boat, still struggling valiantly to stay afloat, her diesel engines on their last legs, ran straight into the mine that Churchill personally had ordered Coastal Command to lay off the entrance to every Norwegian port capable of taking a U-boat. The Train Buster's sank immediately. With all hands...

Book Five

The End Run

One

The great secret government listening and code-deciphering unit at Bletchley Park in the Home Counties was caught completely by surprise at the news of the German decode. It was just in the middle of the night shift changeover. Some 4,000 men and women, military and civilian, who worked there were heading for their homes or the many canteens, coughing and spluttering in the cold night air, adjusting their torches and blacked-out cycle lights, trying to start reluctant motors (those who were entitled to petrol coupons) when it came through. After a long week of virtual silence, the boffins had finally succeeded in decoding the newest form of the German naval code and what a decode it was. Exhausted as the boffins were after working on 'Whale'* for weeks,

*The various German naval codes were given the names of sea creatures – 'Shark', 'Porpoise', etc. – by the scientist trying to break them.

259

they couldn't help but spread the news around those in the camp who had sworn the Ultra Secrecy code, with a revolver aimed at their temples to make the novice decoders well aware of the vital importance of their assignment.

But the news of the tremendous break-through was not restricted to those who had sworn the Ultra Secrecy oath. There were others who had merely sworn to obey the rules of the Official Secrets Act, who also soon became aware that something of great importance had taken place this November night in the year 1942. After all, despite the great pressure put on everyone who worked at Bletchley to 'Keep mum', as the posters warning against careless talk put it, it was virtually impossible to do so. The news of every great decoding breakthrough seemed to crackle through the very air electrically. Jaded and weary as they were that cold drab winter's morning, the Bletchley workers abandoned their breakfasts of watery pow-dered eggs and almost sugarless tea, smok-ing well above their rations of cigarettes and pipe tobacco, to discuss the breakthrough.

All of them, even the charladies who worked in the shabby Nissen huts where the great discoveries were made, knew roughly how the German Enigma coding machines worked and how their codes were broken. Electric current on the squat little Enigma machine flowed from keyboard to lamps. This was achieved by a set of three wired rotors. At least one of these turned a notch every time a key was struck. Each of these rotors was slotted on a spindle with 26 possible starting positions. This meant 17,576 possible combinations for the cryptanalysts to tackle. If that wasn't difficult enough for the boffins, there were sixty potential rotor systems which gave a figure of 1,054,560 possible connections which led through other complicated settings to a potential of *150 million million different starting positions*!

Yet someone had done it with 'Whale'. Indeed, whoever the genius was who had broken the latest German naval code seemed to have done so with remarkable ease. As the insiders and those who knew something of the whole remarkable business on the fringe considered over their stale cigarettes and cold tea in their various canteens, it appeared to them – at first – to have been *too* easy. Were the Jerries attempting to trick them? Was this some kind of feint to lead the U-boat killers up the garden path? But after ten minutes or so (and ten minutes was an age at Bletchley, with the Prime Minister and various service chiefs constantly crying out for the latest information) the Bletchley workers conceded that the decode had to be genuine.

By five, despite the early hour and heavy fog on the road north from London, Admiral Godfrey, head of Naval Intelligence, had arrived personally at Bletchley to make the overwhelming decision: was the message genuine and should the Prime Minister be wakened and told the details of the decode – for the somewhat portly admiral knew the PM would want to decide personally what should be done next.

Restlessly Godfrey listened while the various experts, civilians and officers of Naval Intelligence stationed at Bletchley for emergencies such as this, gave their opinions. Chain-smoking worse than ever, coughing at regular intervals and wishing, despite the earliness of the hour, that he could allow himself a stiff whisky, he decided finally that he had heard enough. Now it was up to him to take the bit between his teeth and decide.

He pushed back his chair noisily. The boffin, who looked a typical don, who was expounding his own particular theory at that moment, stopped immediately. He looked at the red-faced admiral over the top of his pince-nez and quavered in a thin reedy academic type of voice, 'Questions, Admiral?'

'No. Answers, Professor,' Godfrey boomed as if he were back on the quarterdeck of the battle cruiser he had once commanded. 'I've made up my mind. It's genuine and it should go to the PM immediately – and damn the earliness of the hour...'

Churchill could be moody, especially when he was depressed – 'the black dog', as he called it. But despite the fact that it was only just beginning to grow light over the capital and the girls of the WAAF were just starting to raise the barrage balloons in parks throughout London, he received his visitor, immediately and without protest. 'Well, Godfrey,' he demanded as the Admiral was ushered into Number Ten, 'where's the fire?' He dipped the end of his fat cigar into his morning glass of brandy and waited for the Naval Intelligence officer's answer.

As always when he was in the Prime Minister's presence, Godfrey, who had turned many a young officer into a near-trembling wreck in his time as a captain of the battle-cruiser, was flustered. He pulled the decode from his pouch and placed it directly in front of the great man. Churchill looked a little surprised and tried to look stern until he remembered he hadn't put in his false teeth. Hastily he took them out of the glass next to the brandy schooner and thrust them into his mouth. 'Well, what has Bletchley been up to now,' he asked, not looking at the decode, 'that entails robbing an old man of his well-deserved rest?'

Godfrey's plump face went red with embarrassment. 'Sir, Bletchley have unravelled "Whale", and they've come through with something of a sensation.'

'Pray elucidate, Admiral.'

'The decode shows that the Hun has penetrated the Yank, er, American convoy—'

'*What?*' Churchill sat bolt upright, his bantering mood forgotten at once.

'If you read the decode, sir, you'll see the skipper of one of the Hun wolfpack – we believe it's one of their damned aces, a Commander Hartung—'

'Get on with it, Admiral.' Churchill cut him short harshly.

'Has penetrated the convoy's escorts and he is being followed by the rest of those damned ruthless killers of his.' He paused and waited for Churchill's reaction.

Godfrey didn't have to wait long. Churchill reacted almost immediately. 'How did this damned Hartung get away with it?'

'The usual ploy, is our guess. Underneath one of our craft so that the escort's hydrophone operators couldn't distinguish the sub's noise from that of the engines of the Allied ship above her.'

Churchill nodded his understanding. 'Cunning buggers, the Huns,' he remarked. 'All right, so they got a sub – and with more to come perhaps – inside the convoy. The question now is what we're going to do about it, eh?'

'Well, on the way here I have considered the problem. There are two ways to deal with the first sub that has got through. One, we could have the escort's bigger ships, supported by the fleet air arm chaps, attempt to blow the U-boat out of the water.'

'Dangerous,' Churchill objected. 'You know our pilots. They are notoriously inaccurate. They might hit the Yankee ships, and all hell would be let loose if they hit a Yankee tanker.'

'Agreed.'

'So?'

'We seemingly try to deal with the submarine with just one lightly armed craft of the escort, which doesn't have the fire power to harm the American ships even at close quarters. If that craft could lure the U-boat to surface the Hun skipper won't want to waste his torpedoes on such a craft when he has so many tempting larger targets within range – with a bit of luck we could nobble the submarine and—'

'You mean we'd use this lightly armed craft of yours,' Churchill interrupted the Admiral impatiently, 'as a kind of lure – a bait, eh?'

'Yessir,' Godfrey answered, somewhat unhappily, for he guessed what Churchill would say next. 'I suppose one could describe it in that manner.'

'But, Admiral, that would mean sacrificing some of our chaps in order to bring the Huns to the surface – and an escort vessel, too; and since these convoys to Russia have commenced we've lost so many escorts that we cannot afford to lose too many more.'

'Agreed, sir. But remember, sir, you can't make an omelette without cracking eggs.'

'Easily said when you're not one of the eggs,' Churchill quipped. 'No matter. What kind of vessel are you going to use as bait and what is the name of her captain? I need to know these things, Godfrey, if I am going to live with my conscience later.'

That 'later' convinced Godfrey that the PM had already mentally agreed to go along with his rough and ready plan. He answered eagerly. 'Not much to speak of, sir. Just a broken-down old tub of a minesweeper, which should have been scrapped years ago.'

'Her name?'

'The *Black Swan*, known locally in the north, I believe, as the *Mucky Duck*.' He chanced a smile.

Churchill did not respond to it; his face remained set and serious.

'And her skipper? Is he just as broken-down as his ship?'

'I suppose you could say so, sir. He blotted his copybook in North Africa. Something to do with the Vichy French, I believe. Just escaped a court martial, it is said.'

Churchill paused, puffing thoughtfully at his big cigar for a few moments, before saying, 'A useless ship and a handful of useless sailors under the command of a captain, who is equally useless, eh?'

Godfrey flushed again. 'In a way, sir.'

'No loss to the Royal Navy and human-kind?'

Godfrey didn't answer. He felt that Churchill wasn't asking him his opinion, but questioning himself. So he kept his mouth shut and prayed that this awful interview would be ended soon and he could depart into the cold fresh air outside where a convoy of the Bofors anti-aircraft guns, manned by women, were trundling towards Hyde Park where they would take up their defensive positions for the day in case the German airforce attacked again.

It seemed an age before the Quods passed and Churchill finally broke his silence to say, 'All right. So be it, Admiral. Use this, er, *Mucky Duck* of yours, and I hope in years to come that you'll be able to live with your conscience.'

Godfrey didn't venture a comment. Instead he placed on his gold-braided cap hurriedly, saluted and turned, as if he could not get out of the room quickly enough. Behind he left a silent Churchill, two great tears coursing slowly down his chubby cheeks...

Two

'Well, sir, have we done it?' the young petty officer whispered, breaking the heavy silence.

Hartung took his time. He wasn't going to spoil his chances of a massive kill by making any unnecessary noise now. For a while now they had received no asdic 'gravel', the sound like that of someone pouring pebbles, which indicated that asdic operators above them inside the convoy were searching for the U-boat. During that same period his tense sweating hydrophone operators, their faces hollowed out into blood-red death's heads in the subdued light of silent running, had reported no propeller sounds.

He broke his own silence. 'Well, *Obermaat*, there's only one way to find out, isn't there?'

The young petty officer forgot the strain of the last tense hours and forced a youthful grin. 'Take her up, sir?'

'Yes, take her up,' he echoed, and then

snapped, every inch the tough U-boat ace, 'periscope height, please.' All around the ratings tensed at the order.

A hiss of compressed air escaping. The great metal tube slid upwards, while the skipper turned his battered white cap from back to front, so that its brim didn't get in his way when he looked through the periscope.

Slowly, almost painfully, the submarine rose towards the surface. Hartung, using all his experience and know-how, watched, his gaze flashing here, there and everywhere as the U-boat edged its way upwards, while his officers watched the 'trim', as if mesmerized.

'A slight turbulence,' Hartung said hoarsely. 'Periscope height ... trim?'

'Perfect, sir,' one of his officers responded, a nerve ticking electrically at the side of his dirty, unshaven face.

'Thank you.' Hartung approached the periscope. This time he squatted on his knees to take it. By this means he could use the scope at the very minimum height. A moment later the lens broke the surface. Now it pivoted just millimetres above the water. Slowly at low power, Hartung swept the grey swell. He tensed for the first sign of smoke or a masthead in the near distance. That might indicate instant danger. There was not one.

He breathed a sigh of relief. He switched to high power. Straight away normal vision was magnified four times. The area immediately around the scope seemed to leap at him. Still nothing. He swivelled the periscope's handles and turned it upwards so that he could view the hard-blue northern sky. Again nothing. The sky was devoid of aircraft.

Now he took a really long look at the horizon. There they were. The long, plodding line of fat merchantmen, his for the having, if he wished. But Hartung had not survived so long in the U-boat war by taking unnecessary chances. He took in each enemy ship, one by one, judging its deck armament, trying to ascertain if the cunning Tommy swine had infiltrated an escort vessel among the easy targets of the merchant ship. Yes, there she was! He adjusted the focus delicately, his big broad hands altering it with almost female delicacy. He was right. The little craft had twin machine guns behind her bridge and what looked like a modern 40mm Oerlikon cannon at her bow. She was an escort vessel all right and thankfully she hadn't spotted him. She remained on cruise course, keeping pace with the much slower merchantmen, remaining between him and them. 'Like a bloody sheepdog protecting its little baa-lambs,' he commented cynically to himself. He realized as he gave the order to lower the periscope that once he had dealt with the escort the merchantmen were his. But he had to watch his tin fish. He had only so many, and every one of them had to count. He doubted that he'd ever get a juicier target than this again.

He faced his crew and beamed at them. He was happy with them and himself. He knew, and they did, too, that they faced a lot of danger still. All the same, they had a chance now of making a spectacular kill and getting away with it. Then there wouldn't be a crew in the whole of Doenitz's U-boat arm that would be able to match them in achievements.

For a few minutes Hartung indulged himself in a kind of sentimental feeling – one might even call it love – for them. Such a feeling was foreign to his nature, yet he sensed it: a group of brave young men risking their lives in the midst of the enemy camp, with every man's hand against them, for the sake of the Fatherland. Then he pulled himself together, telling himself that a U-boat skipper had no right to be sloppy about such matters.

'Comrades,' he said quite sternly now, 'at the moment we're faced with one single enemy escort vessel. Eliminate it and we have a group of juicy enemy targets for the taking, the like of which I have never seen in the whole of my wartime career.'

He watched their faces as he let the words sink in for a moment. Their happy looks vanished to be replaced by ones of earnest attention.

'Now the escort vessel is swanning around up there as if she is on a peacetime patrol,' he encouraged them, 'seemingly unaware that any kind of danger lurks within five hundred kilometres of her. We shall take advantage of her sloppiness. I can't afford to waste a tin fish on her. We'll surface and hit her with gunfire. Immediately thereafter, before the merchantmen can get a fix on us, we'll submerge, take out as many of those fat tubs of merchantmen as we have torpedoes. Then we beat it.' He paused and waited for someone to ask the overwhelming question that had begun to worry him now that the briefing was over. Fortunately no one did and again he felt a sentimental attachment to his young men; they were not going to trouble him with that question at this official phase of the operation. 'How do we get away when obviously the other escort vessels will have been alerted after the attack?' he asked. 'I'll tell you. We'll fake the old U-boat-sunk trick. You know the drill, comrades. Some of your old duds, a few cans, etc., fired from the torpedo tubes, bilge and some diesel oil. It'll fool the Tommies for a while and then we'll be off back to the Fatherland to a heroes' welcome. There'll be medals for all of you.' He allowed himself a wintry smile. 'And as much juicy gash and good Munich suds as you randy old drunks can cope with. D'yer hear, you bunch o' piss pansies.'

That did it. They broke out into broad smiles, nodding their approval. Hinrichs, the oldest rating on board, sucked his false teeth as if he were already pouring good Munich beer 'behind his collar stud', as he would have put it, and said, 'Them buck-toothed, tea-swilling Tommies'll have to get up a lot earlier in the day to catch us out, skipper.' There was a murmur of agreement from the others and Hartung, seemingly good humoured now, commented, 'and perhaps we'll be able to retire you, Hinrichs, at long last. You've been at this game long enough...'

But as the crew, chatting happily among themselves, went back to their duty posts to prepare for what was to come, *Kapitanleutnant* Hartung was suddenly strangely worried. It all seemed much too easy...

'It's no use, sir,' CPO Tidmus said, his wrinkled old face very worried. 'I can't stop him.' He nodded to the bridge, white and heavy with glittering hoar frost. 'And if you'll forgive me, sir, I don't think you could either.'

Smythe followed the direction of the old petty officer's glance and saw the skipper staggering slightly as he raised the bottle of whisky to his lips. 'I wouldn't even dare try, Chiefie,' he agreed. 'But we haven't seen him like this ... I mean, what's got into the captain?'

'Search me.' Tidmus shrugged his skinny shoulders. 'I think it's that order to keep sailing parallel to the convoy. It goes against the grain. The skipper must think it's totally duff. We're failing in protecting the convoy.'

Smythe nodded, glad of the thickness of the duffle coats which kept at bay some of the icy wind blowing straight down from the Arctic. He, too, couldn't see any purpose to the order which had come, via the convoy commander, straight from the Admiralty itself. As far as he could reason, it made the old *Black Swan* a sitting duck steaming at slow speed together with the convoy instead of moving about back and forth ready for any lurking Jerry U-boat. It was almost, as the fat sailor who had asked permission to grow a beard had complained, as if 'them gold-braided buggers want the squareheads to shove a torpedo up our arse'.

Obviously Commander Donaldson felt the same. Why else was he getting steadily drunker, really incapable of running the old tub? 'But what are we going to do, Chiefie?' Smythe asked.

'I think there's only one way out for us.'

'What's that?'

'Just let him get pissed out of his mind, sir, if you'll forgive my French.'

'And then?' Smythe asked, already knowing the answer and not liking it.

'We'll have to take over, the two of us.' Tidmus pulled a face. 'That's the only way, though it'll be difficult.'

'You mean the bridge?' Smythe asked, feeling a sense of apprehension at the very thought of taking over command of the *Black Swan*.

Tidmus nodded.

'If I may say so, sir, I know you're young and it's a big responsibility taking over a ship with so many matelots' lives depending on you. But the way the captain is now it's better that you do than let him keep on drinking and perhaps make a mistake that'll put us all at risk.'

Up above, in the bridgehouse, Donaldson crashed into the side wall and almost dropped his bottle. He shouted something that they couldn't make out. Smythe thought it might be a curse against the cruel trick that fate had played upon him, turning him from a professional naval officer who had won two medals for bravery into a drunk who couldn't be trusted to run an old tub like the *Black Swan*.

'How long do we wait?' Smythe asked.

Tidmus heaved a sigh. 'I hope not too long, sir. It's very sad to see someone like Commander Donaldson in this state, especially in front of the HO men; they don't have much respect for the Royal Navy as it is. Perhaps he'll pass out soon, and then we can act.' He touched his hands, covered with liver spots, to his cap. 'I'm off, sir. I'll check the lookouts. In this kind of weather they do like to get out of the wind and dodge the column.'

Smythe returned his salute and heard himself say, 'Good thinking, Chiefie.' Then the CPO was gone, leaving the young sub-lieutenant alone with his thoughts.

He knew that the inevitable would happen and, as Donaldson had realized before he had commenced getting drunk after receiving the strange order from the Admiralty, they might well be a sitting target. So, as unhappy about the situation as he was, and inexperienced on top of it, he knew he ought to prepare for an emergency. He'd have a look at the little tub's primitive defences – just in case.

As he wound his way round the ship, he could see just how primitive they were, except for the modern 40mm cannon. The Lewis guns on the 'monkey island' behind the bridge were World War One vintage and lacked the pans of ammunition necessary for substained firing. And the only real defence against air attack, if it came, was the PAC rockets, manned by an elderly three-striper, one of the few regular Royal Navy men on board the *Black Swan*.

As Smythe approached, the man straightened up a little and touched his hand to his cap like some factory worker when he spotted the boss. 'Just getting 'em ready, sir,' he explained without being asked. He warmed his red hands against the stove-like pipe through which the steam came from the engine room to fire the Heath Robinson gadgets, hand grenades contained in tin cans. He grinned showing his yellow false teeth. 'Like a hot tatie cart before the war, sir,' he added. 'You'd think we was offering old Jerry ruddy hot tatie suppers instead of bombs.'

Despite the seriousness of his mood, Smythe grinned. Nothing seemed to get the old hands down. Matelots like the three-striper seemed to take everything in their stride; little appeared to shake them.

'How's the captain, sir, if I may ask, sir?' the old sailor asked. 'I served under him back in '40 at Narvik. He was a real gentleman.' He looked enquiringly at the young sub-lieutenant.

Smythe felt himself blushing as he had done all the time in what seemed another age. 'Oh, all right, I think. Bit under the weather, I think.'

'Yes, that'll be it, sir – a bit under the weather,' the old three-striper agreed loyally.

Smythe touched his hand to his cap and passed on. Behind him the three-striper commenced work again on his primitive weapon, singing to himself as he did so, *'I don't want to set the world on fire ... I just want to start a flame in your heart...'*

The young officer shook his head. With his 'hot tatie cart', he didn't think the old man would set anything on fire, especially not an attacking German.

It was just about then that Bunts came slipping and sliding on the iced-up deck to exclaim excitedly, 'The captain's just passed out, sir, and the lookout reports he's sighted a suspicious object off the port bow.'

Later, it would seem to Smythe that those two reports, uttered in a breathless Scouse accent, were like a clear note of a bugle sounding a call to arms for him personally. The time had come for him to take charge.

Three

Smythe lowered his binoculars as they carried the captain down below to his cabin, still clutching the nearly empty bottle of whisky. He looked at Tidmus grimly, his feelings mixed. Donaldson had let them down by getting drunk like this just when they were in the middle of an emergency. All the same he felt some sympathy for the older officer. Even the dullest member of the crew of the *Black Swan* knew that Commander Donaldson was finished now. He would not be able to cover up this grave dereliction of duty.

'Well, what do you think, Chiefie?' he asked, forgetting the skipper now. 'Do you think what I think?'

'Yessir. I'm pretty sure that it's a sub, and the only subs around here are Jerry ones.'

He raised his glasses once more and adjusted the focus carefully. 'But why surface like that, Chiefie?'

'Usual thing, sir, I suppose. Save torpedoes. They can sink the Yanks with gunfire, if necessary, especially the tankers. They'll go up like tinderboxes if they're hit.'

The long sinister grey shape of the U-boat slid into the circle of calibrated glass, and Smythe thought he could make out the heads peering above the edge of the conning tower. Was one of them the U-boat skipper – another man like himself, but much better trained and – experienced? Yet still a young man with the same dreams and hopes, who might (just as he might) die violently in the next few minutes? He dismissed the thought.

'Chiefie,' he ordered, a sudden new authority in his voice, 'you take the bridge, I'll supervise our fire power, piss-poor as it is.'

Tidmus looked at Smythe. He had never heard the 'snotty' talk in this tough authoritative manner before. He was about to comment, but changed his mind, saying instead, 'Get in the first shot before the squarehead spots us and we could be lucky.'

'Of course.' Smythe pulled up the hood of his duffle coat. 'Here we go.' He laughed and used the well-worn phrase from *ITMA*, as foolish as it seemed: 'Can I do you now, sir.'

The old petty officer's red-rimmed eyes suddenly filled with tears. Under his breath he whispered, 'Best of luck, sir,' and then he concentrated on his task. Down below in his cabin, Commander Donaldson began to sing drunkenly...

For a moment or two, *Kapitanleutnant* Hartung was distracted by the reappearance of the Northern Lights, displaying themselves in that awe-inspiring spectacle. How beautiful that kaleidoscope of brilliant coloured patterns was in this grim black-and-white world of the Arctic. Then he remembered the task at hand. Turning to the man on watch, he yelled above the wind and the roar of the surface water breaking over the U-boat's bow, 'Have you spotted the Tommy yet, Watchman?'

'I had, sir. Now I've gone and lost the arsehole.'

'Well, damn well find the arsehole again – *dalli ... dalli*. I want to get my teeth into those juicy merchantm—'

He never finished the order. There was a blinding flash. Steel struck steel. A mast came tumbling down in a shower of angry blue sparks. The watchman, higher than the skipper, screamed in agony. In that same instant he was catapulted against the back of the conning tower, his back broken immediately. For a moment he hung there, arms outstretched, dying like some latter-day Jesus as the alarm bells started to shrill their urgent warning.

'Heaven, arse and cloudburst!' Hartung cried, throwing up his binoculars once more as red and white tracer shells chased each other across the water at a crazy rate. The battle had commenced. The Tommies had attacked first.

Donald retched miserably and then, unable to stop himself, he vomited over the side of his bunk, the first time he had been sick since he had first gone to sea as a young midshipman in a bygone age. The shock seemed to sober him up a little. He was appalled by vomiting thus and by what he remembered of his behaviour before he had passed out on the bridge. How he had got here to his cabin he did not know. All he realized now with sudden misery was that he was finished, washed up, ready for the beach after their Lordships dismissed him from the service, as they were certain to do.

'No,' he said thickly. 'No, I won't have it.'

He sat up and wished next moment he hadn't. His head spun and for a moment he felt he was going to pass out again on his bunk. Just in time he caught himself, grabbing hold of the battered chest of drawers, which was the spartan cabin's only furniture apart from a battered horsehair chair.

Now he could hear the rapid thump-thump of the forward Oerlikon It penetrated his skull that the *Black Swan* was engaged in some kind of a fight, possibly with the German sub they had been seeking all along. He groaned again. 'You drunken swine,' he said thickly. Here he was, drunk in his cabin, while his teenage HO men, green as the growing grass, were fighting a battle.

He exerted all his strength and pulled himself up by means of the chest of drawers. Holding on with one hand, he edged the top drawer out and picked up the half-bottle of Haig. 'Don't be Vague, Ask for Haig!' His final reserve. With his teeth he pulled out the cork, spat it to the floor and took a hefty slug. The fiery liquid slammed into the back of his throat. He coughed thickly and felt it burn its way down to his guts. He shook his head again. This time he didn't feel like passing out. He levered himself completely upright and, with a hand that shook violently, managed to pull on his battered cap with its green-tarnished gold braid. Through the little porthole, he could see the stabs of purple flame over the sea. The *Black Swan* was being attacked and he had to do something about it. He forced open the heavy metal door and stepped shakily into the open. If he was going to die now, it was the best thing that could happen to him; it would be an honourable death in battle with the enemy. He staggered on, ready now for the inevitable.

'Bearing green three-oh,' Smythe yelled as the smoke cleared to reveal that their first salvo had badly peppered the U-boat's superstructure. There were gleaming silver scars, caused by the shrapnel, all along her conning tower and one of her masts was hanging down, trailing wires in the water behind her. 'Range fifteen hundred ... Deflection – zero!'

The HO men who manned the quick-firer needed no urging. They knew the U-boat outgunned the *Mucky Duck* and at a pinch the German skipper would use his torpedoes. It was up to them to see off the Jerry before he saw them off.

'*FIRE!*'

Behind the bridge on the monkey island the Lewis gunner opened up, pouring tracer towards the U-boat to act as a guide for the forward deck gunners, who opened up the very next instant.

The 40mm shells sped towards the U-boat in a lethal fury. Steaming yellow shell cases poured from the Oerlikon, melting the ring of ice on the deck below into a wet mist. Hastily the gunner's mate slapped new shell cases into the great maws of the foreign cannon, while Smythe watched through his binoculars, trying his utmost to keep his balance on the heaving deck, knowing that he'd have to knock the U-boat out soon before her gunners got the *Black Swan*'s range and there was all hell to pay.

On the submarine's deck men were crumpling into shapeless heaps. Here and there Germans were swept over the side by that tremendous volume of fire, as if they were pitiful flies swatted by some gigantic hand. Others ran back and forth along the forrard deck, waving their arms wildly, whether in surrender or anger, Smythe could not tell.

But already the German submarine was preparing to fight back. Sheltering behind the shield of the deck 75mm cannon, the German gunners were swinging their weapon round frantically. Without looking behind him, Smythe yelled to the rating manning the Lewis gun on the monkey island. 'Those gunners – knock the buggers out. NOW!' Despite the freezing cold, the beads of sweat were streaming down his forehead, threatening to blind Smythe as he peered through his glass at the German vessel. But there was no response from behind him. Angrily Smythe turned. The Lewis gunner stood slumped over his antiquated machine gun, his face looking as if someone had thrown a handful of strawberry jam at it, dead.

But Smythe had no time to consider the fate of the young gunner for staggering down the narrow stretch of deck in front of the bridge, hanging on to every hold, there came Commander Donaldson, obviously drunk still, but with his battered old cap set at the regulation angle, as if he were trying to sober up and act the role of skipper once again.

'Sir!' Smythe cried.

Donaldson waved his hand at him, as if the young sub-lieutenant might try to stop him. 'Leave me be, Lieutenant,' he said thickly. 'I'm all right ... I can manage.' To prove himself, or so it seemed, he grabbed hold of the icy-white ladder that led up to the bridge, where CPO Tidmus was desperately swinging the wheel to left and right, zigzagging the best he could, trying to dodge the fire that surely would be soon coming from the U-boat.

For a moment Smythe didn't know what to do; he felt completely out of his depth. But instinctively he knew he would have to do something. Tidmus was fully occupied on the bridge, his firepower had already been reduced by half and now the drunken skipper was seemingly trying to take over once more. But could he allow him to do so in his present condition?

The decision was taken from him the next moment. With the Lewis gunner now dead, the German gunlayers manning their 75mm cannon acted without fear of being mown down by the Tommy machine guns. They fired. *Crack!* Scarlet flame stabbed the intervening distance, as Smythe yelled frantically to his own gunners, 'Concentrate on the bridge ... For fuck's sake, *concentrate your fire on the sub's bridge, men!*' Even as he gave the desperate order, he realized he had sworn in public for the first time in his young years and was shocked by the knowledge.

But there was no time now to concentrate on the morality of using obscene words, for the first 75mm German shell slammed into the wheelhouse in the same moment that Smythe's own gun crew flayed the U-boat's deck and conning tower with 40mm shells.

Ratings went down, their twisting bodies splashed with bright-red blood. Hot slivers of steel flew everywhere. Next to Hartung, a lookout reeled back, holding his eye, blood spurting through his tightly clenched fingers. Hartung himself yelped as something burning hot plunged into his left shoulder like the thrust of a red-hot poker. He staggered, but caught himself just in time. He was in command. Everything depended upon him. He couldn't afford to succumb to a wound.

Brain working at top speed and with electric precision, Hartung worked out what to do next. Already the merchantmen would have spotted him. The crazy firefight would have alerted them to the danger – and his position. Even the green *Amis* would already be signalling the outer escorts what was going on. He had to get rid of the lone escort immediately and then concentrate on sinking as many of the merchantmen as he had torpedoes.

He grabbed the voice tube. 'Both ahead,' he yelled above the blast of the U-boat's cannon. He followed the order as the submarine picked up speed almost immediately. 'Full power astern. Wheel hard over ... *Full ahead!*'

The U-boat responded beautifully. Now she was presenting the smallest possible target for the Tommy gunners, as she sped forward, a white bone in her teeth. Without even being ordered to, the deck gun crew reacted to the changed position, swinging their gun round on to the target within seconds and firing the very next instant. Now the distance between the two unequal opponents closed swiftly, with the advantage now on the side of the better-armed submarine. Despite the burning pain of his wound, the warm blood trickling down his arm under his leather jacket, Hartung grinned. The Tommy was doomed. Then the slaughter of the damned boastful Americans who thought they could come to Europe and do what they damned well liked would commence. He braced himself for what was to come, the epitome of the Nazi warrior, blond, arrogant and confident that Germany under its Führer Adolf Hitler would conquer the world.

Donaldson was taken completely by surprise. The shell caught him just as the German shell slammed into the wheelhouse.

For one long moment he thought he was still drunk and had overbalanced, then in that last instant as his body disintegrated in a welter of blood, gore and broken bone he knew he hadn't; he had failed. Then he was dead.

CPO Tidmus wasn't – yet. He lay gasping, as if he had just run a long race, among the ruins of the bridge, what seemed a heavy weight pinning him down to the deck, a thin red mist threatening to envelop him at any moment. He choked and vomited down the front of his uniform. Somehow the act of retching and vomiting cleared the mist away. He forced his head up, the blood running down the left side of his old face, and stared at the wreck of the bridge. At the same time he noticed that the *Black Swan* was still moving and that far, far away, or so it seemed, her Oerlikon was still firing. He saw, too, that something strange had happened to his body.

It had seemingly grown shorter. He believed he frowned then, though he couldn't be sure, for he could really not feel any movement, even that of his facial muscles. With a bit of an effort, spitting out the rest of the vomit, he raised his head a little higher. Yes, he was definitely shorter. Why?

Then he had it. Opposite, mingled with the smoking debris of the wrecked bridge were two legs. Without any particular surprise he recognized them as his. He was sure of that. He remembered their fur-lined boots. His missus had bought them for him on Hull's black market the previous Christmas. He hadn't liked them and had protested, 'But they're not regulation, you silly old moo. You ought to know that – you've been married to me long enough. You can't expect a chief petty officer with thirty years' service behind him to wear non-regulation footwear. They could put me on the rattle for something like that...'

The thought of that year's Christmas died away. A thin pale liquid that wasn't blood started to seep from between his slack lips. Still he continued to stare at the severed legs as if they were an object of some wonder, even mystery to him.

It was thus that an ashen-faced Smythe found him just about to die. He raised the old CPO's head and his false teeth almost popped out of his suddenly slack mouth. 'Chiefie,' he uttered.

Tidmus looked up at him through the mist that was now about to engulf him. 'I did my best—' He stopped short. His head lolled to one side and his false teeth fell to his chest. He was dead.

For a moment Smythe couldn't move. He was all alone now. Both Donaldson and poor old CPO Tidmus had gone. What was he to do? Why should he have such an awesome responsibility thrust upon him at his age? Then it came to him. Why and how he could never recall.

With his elbow he shoved out the remaining glass shards of the bridge window and yelled above the racket made by the cannon, as the U-boat bent on the destruction of the *Black Swan* came ever closer, 'You with the tatie supper cannon!'

'Sir?' The three-striper swung round urgently, alarmed by the new skipper's cry.

'Get that bloody grenade-launcher of yours ready – toot-sweeet.'

'Sir?'

'I want you to fire at my command and for God's sake make sure you hit the target the very first time. We won't get a second chance.'

Obviously the old three-striper was puzzled, but then in his long years in the Royal Navy he had often been puzzled by the ways of the gentlemen of the quarterdeck. So he did what he was told to do. Hurriedly he started to slot in the tin cans containing the grenades, checking that the steam, which would act as a propellant, was working. It was. That made him happy. Three-stripers of his kind always liked things to be in good order and working. Despite the murder and mayhem all around him, he started to sing the current hit of that year so long ago: *'I've got spurs that jingle jangle jingle ... as I go riding merrily along...'*

Smythe forgot the three-striper and his plaintive Yankee cowboy song. Suddenly he was imbued by a new spirit. The adrenaline surged through his bloodstream. Abruptly he felt more confident than he had ever done in his young life before. It was as if the spirit and tradition of young men of his background and class had taken hold of him, making him forget his fears and inhibitions.

It was the sharp, crisp orders of the naval barracks, the stamp of heavy marine boots on the gravel, the sweet clear notes of the bugle – and more. It was the feeling that he came from a long line of young men like himself who had felt that they were part of something more important than just themselves. It was an ill-defined feeling, more a kind of spiritual warmth, which made young men believe that there was something greater than they which made it worthwhile sacrificing their life for.

Now, forgetting everything else, he seized the wheel, still wet with poor Tidmus's blood, and cried down the tube, 'Give me all you've got. *FULL AHEAD!*'

Four

'*Amerikansi ... Slava Amerika ...* !' the crowd, mostly women, cheered and waved, jumping up and down in the snow with excitement as the American ships came steaming slowly to their berths, where grim-faced half-starved prisoners under guard waited to unload their precious supplies.

Smythe, head bandaged, arm in a sling, watched, a little bewildered by it as he stood on the bridge of the Russian tug towing what was left of the *Black Swan* to her own berth.

Next to him the tall blonde skipper spat over the side of her tug and exclaimed in good English, 'Whores ... Murmansk whores!' She spat again in disgust as one of the female welcoming committee lifted up her skirt to reveal she was naked beneath it. The American seamen whooped and yelled with delight and started tossing packs of Camels and Chesterfields on to the quay, causing the women to scramble and fight in the snow for the precious cigarettes, which Smythe had been told would bring a fortune on the Murmansk black market. After all Russian cigarettes, their *paparossi* were made of evil-smelling coarse black tobacco wrapped up in old newspaper. As the female skipper, tall, blonde and well-built, gave her orders to the tug's engine room and it started to slow down even more, she shook her head and added, 'You have deserved better, my friend.'

Smythe blushed, though he thought he would have got over the bad habit by now. But then it wasn't every day that he was praised by a pretty woman who was obviously interested in him, though he couldn't think why. For as the escort commodore had said to him the day before when they had first entered the safety of Russian waters, 'My God, Smythe, you really have been through the wars. You look like someone who's been dragged through a hedge *back-wards.*' Then he had held out his big hand and said warmly, 'But good show, Smythe. You certainly deserve that DSC I've recommended you for.' He had beamed at the battered-looking younger officer and then cried, 'Steward, bring this officer a pink gin – a large one, he certainly deserves it.'

Thereafter everyone in the commodore's wardroom had been slapping his back and offering him pink gins – large ones – as he had to repeat his tale; how he had sunk the German U-boat at the very last instant using the Heath Robinson 'hot tatie cannon'. 'Amazing!' they had chortled, delighted with his account of how the old three-striper, now promoted to petty officer with a DCM in the offing, once the Admiralty had approved, had lobbed three sets of grenades neatly into the German submarine's conning tower just as it was about to slam into the side of the *Black Swan,* now drifting and out of control, its rudder shot away. Time and time again, the young snotties of the command ship had asked, 'And what happened then, Sub-Lieutenant?'; and he had replied gravely, noting that respectful 'sub-lieutenant', 'She simply went under. Flooded instantly, I suppose.' And they had looked at a bloody Smythe as if he were some fabulous alien creature from another world.

Now, as the survivors of the one-sided battle prepared to throw their land lines to the waiting Russian prisoners on the quay, shaven heads bowed in submission, the tug's skipper took off her fur cap and shook her head so that her blonde tresses cascaded down to her shoulders. *'Davoi,'* she commanded. 'Come. No more cheap whores. We go to my cabin. We drink vodka.' And she had looked at him sternly but significantly, as if she intended to offer him more than a glass of vodka.

And she did! 'By God, didn't she half!' he would relate when he was an old man and retired rear-admiral, who had made love to women all over the world. 'Black, brown, yellow, you name the colour, I've had 'em all,' he would boast with a naughty twinkle in his faded blue eyes.

'So it all ended well, Smythie?' his old cronies would remark years later when they would relax over port and walnuts after dinner at the rundown manor house he had managed to buy down in Hampshire.

He would pause before answering, remembering himself and the Russian woman, whose name he had long forgotten, thrashing about on her narrow bunk as she took his virginity, pumping herself up and down on his bruised skinny young body, yelling in her sexual frenzy in Russian, while he told himself he had become a man at last. 'I suppose you could say so,' he would then reply slowly and a little thoughtfully. 'Well for me, old friends.'

They would fall silent for a few moments, their lined old faces hollowed out to skulls in the flickering yellow light of the candles set along the long polished table, and he would tell himself they were dying men; there'd be ever fewer of them alive when they came together to celebrate Trafalgar Day next year.

'But as for the others,' he would continue slowly, trying to remember the faces of those long dead men of the old *Mucky Duck*, which vanished below the surface of the harbour at Murmansk the day after she had completed that terrible Murmansk Run. As time had passed it had become increasingly difficult for him do so. But now and again he would recall them as they had been then, those HO youths, products of the Depression, who could be his grandsons now. Then, in the manner of old warriors remembering the dramatic events of their youth and all that sacrifice, his eyes would flood with tears and he would have to hobble away on his stick and cry in the solitude of his study.

But as always his mood of depression and sadness at the losses of the past would vanish. The drink would have its effect – it was surprising just how much these old warriors could still tuck away – and he would raise his glass and intone the toast that the long dead Chiefie, Alf Tidmus, had taught him back in 1942. 'From Hell, Hull and Halifax, may the Good Lord preserve us.'

And his old comrades would don the white berets that marked them as veterans of the Russian convoys and echo that old saying of those who had sailed from Hull all those years before and braved the hell of that Murmansk Run: *'From Hell, Hull and Halifax, may the Good Lord preserve us...'*